Two Lines

World Writing in Translation

Issue 29, Fall 2018

Two Lines Press

SUBSCRIPTIONS
Two Lines is published twice annually.
Subscriptions are $15 per year; individual issues are $12. To subscribe, visit:
www.twolinespress.com

BOOKSTORES
Two Lines is distributed by
Publishers Group West. To order,
call: 1-866-400-5351

TWO LINES
Issue 29
ISBN 978-1-931883-78-8
ISSN 1525-5204

582 Market Street, Suite 700
San Francisco, CA 94104
www.twolinespress.com
twolines@catranslation.org

This project is supported in part by an award from the National Endowment for the Arts.

ART WORKS.
arts.gov

Editor's Note

My roots were somewhere with you,
and only the strange horses loved my whinny, those who belong to no land.
—Nahid Arjouni, translated by Shohreh Laici

I could probably read only authors from Vermont from now until I die and never run out of good books. So, I'm always wary of publishing a group of writers from one country and mistakenly giving the impression that that sliver should be somehow representative of the whole. As if a group of five or nine or a hundred writers could give even an inkling of what a country's literary culture, let alone its history, might be, and as if understanding a literature is even possible.

Americans are familiar with the poetry of Bashō or Issa. Some of you likely know Hiromi Itō or Chika Sagawa or Kiwao Nomura, but there's so much we just don't have access to. In this issue we have a special section devoted to contemporary Japanese poets who haven't had a book in English before. These are poets writing anything, from lyrics to eco-poetic epics. They are all very unique, and many writers exist in the spaces between and outside of their interests—I hope in the next issue and the next we can bring some of those writers to English, too. Never arriving at a whole, but always expanding.

Also in this issue we continue our exploration of world literature, including arresting writing from Iran, Bolivia, Hungary, and elsewhere. And, as is our usual approach, we're not trying to *define* what international literature is, but to explore possibilities, see some new viewpoints, perhaps see that there is literature different from anything we've read before, and, to say as Jaime Sáenz, translated by Ted Dodson, says: "In the end, I worship clear voices..."

CJ EVANS

Fiction

Poetry

The Japanese Vanguard

RITA INDIANA is a Dominican music composer, producer, and key figure in contemporary Caribbean literature; *Tentacle* won the Grand Prize of the Association of Caribbean Writers in 2017, the first Spanish-language book to do so. She is the author of three collections of stories and four novels, and is a driving force in experimental Dominican popular music along with her band, Rita Indiana y los Misterios.

La mucama de Omicunlé

La habitación de Acilde en casa de Esther es uno de esos cuartuchos obligatorios de los apartamentos del Santo Domingo del siglo XX, cuando todo el mundo tenía una sirvienta que dormía en casa y, por un sueldo por debajo del mínimo, limpiaba, cocinaba, lavaba, cuidaba niños y atendía los requerimientos sexuales clandestinos de los hombres de la familia. La explosión de las telecomunicaciones y las fábricas de zona franca crearon nuevos empleos para estas mujeres que abandonaron sus esclavitudes poco a poco. Ahora, los cuartos del servicio, como se lleman, son utilizados como almacenes u oficinas.

Este trabajo le había caído del cielo. Sus rondas en el Mirador apenas le daban para comer y pagar su servicio de datos, sin el que no hubiese podido vivir. Durante su turno activaba el PriceSpy para ver las marcas y los precios de lo que llevanban puestos sus clientes y cobrarles el servicio con aquello en mente. Para las horas de trabajo preparaba un playlist que terminaba siempre con "Gimme! Gimme! Gimme!" de ABBA. Al final de la noche se retaba a conseguir un cliente, darle el servicio y cobrar antes de que la versión en vivo de la canción terminara. Cuando lo lograba se premiaba con un plato de raviolis cuatro quesos en El Cappuccino, una trattoria trattoria a unas cuantas cuadras del Parque. Allí ordenaba en el pobre italiano que aprendía online durante las horas muertas del Mirador e imaginaba . . .

Translated by
ACHY OBEJAS

Tentacle

Acilde's room at Esther's was one of those typical rooms found in Santo Domingo's twentieth-century apartments, when everybody had a servant who lived with them and, for a salary well below minimum wage, cleaned, cooked, washed, watched the kids, and attended to the clandestine sexual requirements of the men of the house. The explosive growth in telecommunications and factories in the Free Trade Zone had created new jobs for these women who had fled their bondage, one by one. Now, these service rooms—as they were called—were used for storage or as offices.

This job had come like a gift from heaven. Her rounds up at the Mirador had barely paid for food and data, without which she couldn't live. During her turns up there, she'd switch on the PriceSpy to check out the brands and prices of her clients' wardrobes, charging them for her services with that in mind. For her working hours, she'd prep a playlist that always ended with ABBA's "Gimme! Gimme! Gimme!" At the end of the night, she'd challenge herself to find a client, service him, and get paid before the live version of the song was over. When she did it, she'd reward herself with a plate of four-cheese ravioli at El Cappuccino, a trattoria a few blocks from the park. She'd order in the poor Italian she'd learned online during dead time at the Mirador and imagine whole conversations with the guys who ate at

El Cappuccino every day, Italians in shoes that cost more than three digits who talked about business and soccer.

In her mind, one of them, a friend of her father's, recognized her, seeing the family resemblance. But that was pure bullshit. Her father had stayed by her mother's side just long enough to get her pregnant. Jennifer, her mother, a brunette with good hair who'd gone to Milan with a modeling contract, had gotten hooked on heroin and ended up selling her ass on the metro in Rome. She'd had six abortions when she decided to go through with the seventh pregnancy, returning to her homeland so she could dump the baby on her parents, two bitter peasants from Moca who'd moved to the city after La Llorona and the two years of rain that had destroyed their homestead forever.

They beat Acilde as they liked, for being a tomboy, for wanting to play ball, for crying, for not crying. She'd compensate for the beatings at school with whoever glanced her way, and whenever she fought she'd lose track of time and a reddish light would fill her line of vision. In time, her knuckles swelled from the many scars forged from going against foreheads, noses, and walls. She had the hands of a man but that wasn't enough: she wanted the rest.

Her family detested her masculine ways. The grandfather, César, decided to cure the granddaughter, bringing over a young neighbor to see to her while he and the grandmother held her down and an aunt covered her mouth. That same night, Acilde ran away from home. She asked Peri, the class faggot, if she could sleep at his place, a studio on Roberto Pastoriza, like the kind Peri's mom, Doña Bianca, rented out to students from the village. The day of the tidal wave, Acilde went down to the Mirador, along with thousands of others who were curious or who'd managed to escape still in their pajamas; she wanted to see how that terrible wave had swallowed her grandparents in their smelly little apartment in the Cacique.

Peri knew entire dialogues from twentieth-century comedies no one had seen, like *Police Academy* and *The Money Pit*. In these movies, Acilde saw the slow life of fifty years ago, and it surprised her that people lived without an integrated data plan or anything. Kids from well-off homes dropped in at Peri's to take pills and, sometimes for several days in a row, to play the *Giorgio Moroder Experience*. The Sony game let you go to a 1977 disco party and dance with other *fevers*, what the kids who preferred war games used to call the millions who went to the virtual party, combining the trip with pills to succumb to the palpitating, sensual synthesizer of "I Feel Love" by Donna Summer, which lasted a whole hour. By dawn, when the pills were gone as well as the money to buy them, Peri and his friend Morla would organize a stroll to the Mirador and, after a few hours of work, they'd come back for the second half of the party.

Morla was a kid from the neighborhood. He studied law and trafficked in whatever was available: fruit trees, those drugs that were still illegal, and marine creatures, a luxury coveted by wealthy collectors now that the three disasters had finished off practically every living thing under the sea. Morla's dream was to work for the government; he lied about his background in front of Peri's other friends, children of bureaucrats who looked down on him when, using their PriceSpys, they confirmed his Versace shirts were knockoffs. It was Morla who first talked to Acilde about Rainbow Brite, an injection doing the rounds in alternative science circles that promised a complete sex change without surgery of any kind. The process had been compared to cold turkey, although the homeless transsexuals who'd served as guinea pigs said it was much worse. In that instant, the fifteen thousand dollars needed for the drug became Acilde's only goal: she had to make that money. And since nothing better had occurred to her, that same night she went with Peri and Morla to the Mirador.

●●●

ONE NIGHT, RIGHT AFTER FINISHING her workout, Acilde heard a hum coming from the room where they kept the altar to Yemayá, the goddess of the sea Omicunlé was devoted to. Esther was sleeping. Acilde dared to go in. It smelled of incense and flower-scented water, of old fabric and the smell of the sea contained inside conch shells. She approached the altar whose centerpiece was a replica of a Greek vase some three feet tall. Eric liked to kid Esther that someday he'd inherit it; Acilde knew from her PriceSpy it was worth a bomb. On the central band of the jar was an image of a woman holding a boy by the ankle, who stood by a pool of water she was going to submerge him in. All over the vase there were offerings and the attributes of the goddess: an old oar, a ship's wheel, a feathered fan. Esther had told her never to open the vase, that whoever looked inside without being initiated into the sect would go blind, or some other crazy thing like that. But inside, perfectly illuminated and oxygenated by a mechanism adapted to the jar, Acilde saw a live sea anemone. Without putting the lid back she looked around the bottom border of the vase to find the red eye that responded to the remote control and a small hole where a battery charger would fit perfectly. That's what the old lady was doing when she "attended" to these saints, monitoring the salt levels in the tank where she kept an illegal and very valuable specimen alive. When Acilde tried to use the PriceSpy on the animal, it just loaded endlessly. It didn't work very well with black market prices.

During the transaction that produced Acilde, her father had told her mother he wanted to get to know the Dominican beaches. Back then the island was a tourist destination with coasts full of coral, fish, and anemones. She brought her right thumb to the center of her left palm to activate the camera, and flexing her index finger she photographed the creature, then she flexed her middle finger to send the photo to Morla. She whispered a question to caption the image: "How much would they give us for this?"

Morla's response was immediate: "Enough for your Rainbow Brite."

Their little plan was very simple. When the old lady left on a trip, Morla would find a way to get around the building's security, to disconnect the cameras, take the anemone away in a special container, and leave Acilde tied, gagged, and free of any blame. But when Esther left for a conference on African religions in Brazil, Eric stayed in the house. At first, Acilde thought the witch didn't trust her, but later she understood the anemone needed special care, which Eric would dispense in her absence. That was confirmed when she saw how he spent so many dead hours holed up in the saint's room.

On her return, Esther found Eric sick, with diarrhea, the shivers, and a strange discoloring on his arms. She sent him home.

"He asked for it, that bugger," she told Acilde. "Don't take his calls."

Despite Omicunlé's warnings, Acilde visited Eric while he was sick to bring him food and the medicine he prescribed to himself. Eric stayed in his room, where a stink of vomit and liquor reigned. There were days when he was delirious, when he sweated terrible fevers, and when he continually called out to Omicunlé: "Oló! Kun fun me lo mo, oló kun fun."

When Acilde returned to Esther's she did everything she could to try to soften her up: all she managed was to get the old lady to curse him even more, calling him a traitor, dirty, a half-wit.

All the while Morla was sending Acilde desperate texts every day, trying to find out when Esther was leaving the house, when they would carry out their operation, and when, finally, he could get his hands on that anemone. Acilde had stopped answering him.

Every Thursday afternoon a helicopter would pick Esther up from the roof of the apartment building and take her to the national palace to throw shells for the president. The consultation usually went on past midnight because the priestess would make the sacrifices and carry out the cleansings that the shells recommended that same day. These absences seemed perfect for Acilde's original plan, but recently the old lady had said and done things that had convinced her otherwise.

Esther had brought her a blue bead necklace from Brazil; it was consecrated to Olokun, the oldest deity in the world, the sea itself.

"Master of the unknown," Esther explained when she put it on her. "Wear it always because, even if you don't believe, it will protect you. One day, you're going to inherit my house. You won't understand this now, but one day you will."

Omicunlé would get very serious and Acilde would feel very uncomfortable. She couldn't help but feel affection for the old woman who took care of her with a tenderness her own family had never shown her. Plus, if she was going to let her inherit the house, couldn't she also, perhaps, give her money for the sex change?

When the doorbell's wave sounds again, Acilde uses the broom to sweep away the spiderwebs that have silently spun every day in the corners of the ceiling. She assumes it's another Haitian and the security mechanism will take care of him. But then there's a knock on the apartment door. Only Eric, who has the code for the downstairs gate, could have come up. Without any fear that Esther might get mad, she runs to open the door, happy that Eric is well and sure that with his cleverness he will soon charm the priestess again.

Morla points a pistol at her. Acilde makes a move to defend herself but Morla touches her between her collarbones, pressing his fingers together to get access to her operating system. He activates both eyes, in full screen mode, to bring up two different videos: in one eye, "Gimme! Gimme! Gimme!"

and, in the other, "Don't Stop 'til You Get Enough," turning both up as loud as they will go. Acilde tries to disconnect herself. Morla is too quick for her.

Blind, she screams: "*Madrina*, thief!" hitting herself against the walls until she falls to the ground and feels, after a timid shot from a silenced revolver, the weight of another body falling on the marble floor.

Morla deactivates the screens. Acilde watches as he finishes off Esther. She sees him wipe off the sweat that runs down his forehead with the back of the hand that holds the gun.

"You left me hanging, cocksucker, where is the shit?"

Morla doesn't need the empathy of his little group of useless friends anymore; the voice of the man behind the gun is not the same as the one he used to use at Peri's house. Acilde leads him to the saints' room and shows him the giant jar. He opens the cylindrical container he will transport his new merchandise in, sleepless, shaking, and off his tits on coke.

"You should do another line to get yourself together," Acilde advises him.

Morla agrees, pulling out a little pink plastic bag with a piece of rock from his pocket. With a single circular motion, Acilde breaks a Lladró dolphin she's taken from the altar on his head. Morla falls on his side. The design of gold coins on his shirt is sprinkled with blood and bits of porcelain. Acilde puts the anemone in Morla's cylinder and presses the button, activating the oxygen and the temperature the animal needs to survive.

Condylactis gigantea

On her way from Esther's house, Acilde had avoided official taxis and the metro, where cameras would follow her, and taken a ride in a jalopy. These old cars—Japanese models from the early years of the century—were still on the streets in spite of government efforts to pull them from circulation. Their reasonable price and privacy made them ideal for fugitives and the undocumented. The drivers knew the alleys up in the high part of the city and would detour from their routes for a bit more money. Villa Mella, where she'd asked the driver to take her, was the cradle of the evangelical terrorist movement that had emerged after President Bona had declared the 21 Divisions, with its blend of African deities and Catholic saints, as the official religion. The Servants of the Apocalypse, as the enemies of all that was not biblical called themselves, liked to place explosives and kill people almost as much as speaking in tongues. Acilde figured the police wouldn't take long to find her and she'd only find refuge for a few days among those who thought Esther Escudero was an object of demonic adoration and deserved to die.

In the Kemuel commune, an assembly praised God's name with loudspeakers and encouraged believers to help bring about Armageddon on the island. Acilde bet they'd probably already seen her on the web, where her photo would have been shown next to Morla's, and blamed her for the crime. She approached two girls wearing tangled braids and floor-length skirts and asked to be taken to one of their leaders. In the office of Melquesidec, a pastor with sausage-like fingers, there was a desk, two folding chairs, and some faded and stained cushions on a bed of newspapers, from when they still used to print on paper, that was serving as a couch. On the wall, hanging off a single nail, there was a belt with a knife from the mountain. Next to it, a poster read: "And the angel threw his sickle to earth, and harvested the vine of the earth, and threw the grapes into the great winepress of God's anger."

Melquesidec ordered her to sit. *Lies*, thought Acilde, *are like beans, they have to be well seasoned or no one will swallow them*. She made up a dream with a lamb on an altar whose blood formed the letters of Esther Escudero's name. She added things she remembered from the Sunday school her aunt had made her attend as a child. The minister who'd taught those classes was even more hated than Melquesidec; his dealings with girls of twelve and thirteen had put a price on his head. Melquesidec fixed his reddened eyes on Acilde with an otherworldly lust that made her feel more sorry for him than for her clients at the Mirador. "Little sister, the Lord has anointed you and I must protect his work," he said, scratching a nipple with the nail of his pinky. He ordered Brother Sofonías, a young man with a mild case of Down syndrome, to make her feel at home. Before Acilde could stand, Melquesidec had stuck a spit-covered finger in her ear.

Sofonías was very tall, and his tiny eyes were shiny with a false happiness; like everyone else in that place, he smelled like a dirty toilet. The commune took up several blocks, made up of ad hoc houses of wood, zinc, and, sometimes, cement. They had water and electricity irregularly, just like in all the neighborhoods outside the central circuit, where not even the collectors bothered to come. He took her by the arm to a one-roomed shanty with a dirt floor and pushed her inside. He closed the three-planked door and locked it from the outside. She heard him drag a plastic chair over to the front of the door and drop into it with a deep sigh. Inside, alone, Acilde looked around without taking off her backpack, which had the anemone in it. The room would have been perfect for keeping a dog or a woman who was very frightened, but Acilde tested a plank of plywood that made up the wall at the back of the room, and without needing to kick it twice the rotted wood fell apart, creating a hole she could escape through without too much noise. All the while, Sofonías sang: "To the battle march with firm conviction/ behind Christ, our Captain/our hearts swollen with manly ardor/ to defeat Satan's army."

> *Eric got the message: Acilde was in Villa Mella, in deeper than the Titanic...*

Leaping over streams of black water, she ran away from the commune until she reached an avenue where a group of little kids was selling crack to the cars lined up to buy. She went up to the youngest in the group and, using money as bait, got him to take her home with him. He lived with his pregnant sister, who was sitting in front of a pedestal fan eating a plate of rice and salami when they arrived. "I'm not gonna fuck anybody, Joel, I'm eating," Samantha said, hitting the plate with her fork. Without mentioning the bills in his pocket, Joel stuck his hand in her plate and grabbed a piece of sausage. "Just looking for a place to crash," he said.

Acilde saw there was a tablet on a little table in the middle of the room; as soon as she'd left Esther's house, she'd disconnected her data plan so she couldn't be located, but now she needed to reach Eric, the only person who could help her. The tablet was an old model that ran on an independent plan only offered on the city's periphery. Samantha made a move to grab it back but Acilde explained, typing on the screen, that she only needed it for a few minutes. "What, now we're a five-star hotel, asshole?" asked the girl as she disappeared with a plate of plantain behind the little curtain that separated the kitchen and the sitting room. Joel showed Acilde the only bedroom, which had a twin bed. "And your sister?" Acilde whispered, busy with the tablet. But Joel was already in the kitchen, serving himself whatever had been left on the stove.

Acilde sent Eric a picture of a monkey. Eric sent back a photo of the Titanic. Acilde responded with a photo of the Titanic at the bottom of the sea and a photo of a rainbow. After a minute more of photos, Acilde had sent him one of Pancho Villa, one of Matías Mella, another of Mama Tingó, and one of a postcard of a sunset on the beach from back when the sea reflected the sky and wasn't just contaminated chocolate. The monkey was still the most well-known call for help. Even the police knew what it meant. Eric got the message: Acilde was in Villa Mella, in deeper than the Titanic, she had the sea creature with her, and she would return it to him in exchange for Rainbow Brite. She'd wait for him around the Mama Tingó metro station after dark.

I didn't kill her," Acilde said as soon as they were alone. "That's not important now. I'm going to help you with the shot. You can't do it yourself." Acilde was surprised by this reaction; maybe his illness had finally done him in. He pulled out five IVs, gauze and clamps, several bottles, and a piece of cascarilla Esther had used to trace white lines on doors and in the corners of her apartment.

He ordered Acilde to give herself an enema, take a bath, and shave her vulva and head. She did everything with a little shaver, thinking all the while *this guy's a doctor, he knows what he's doing*. He made her lie down on the bed, over which he'd erected a kind of white tent to keep the space around her body sterile. There was a plate of uncooked rice at the foot of the bed. "You're getting pretty folkloric," Acilde said, anxiously watching as Eric pulled a sealed metallic envelope out of a jacket pocket. He tore the envelope with his teeth. "They're offerings so everything will go smoothly," he explained, showing her a vial with about two inches of a white and viscous liquid in it. "It'd better work, cuz it cost me my right ball," he said as he filled a syringe that danced in his hand. When he showed Acilde some latex belts, she sprang up from the bed. "I'm just following instructions," he said and cackled as he touched what would be the patient's new balls. Relieved, Acilde lay back down and let him tie her with the belts. "Try to break loose," he said. She struggled but couldn't move.

Before beginning, Eric took a quick look at the jar where the sea anemone rested. It was in bad shape, like him, and he'd have to act fast. As soon as the Rainbow Brite entered her blood stream, Acilde began to convulse. *I've killed her*, thought Eric. *They sold me rat poison!* But she soon stabilized and he checked her vital signs regularly. Two hours later she complained about the heat and later still told him she was burning alive. When the bed began to shake from her tremors, Eric gave her a sedative. At midnight her small breasts began to fill with smoky bubbles as her mammary glands consumed themselves, leaving a wrinkled knot that looked like gum around her nipple, which Eric removed with pincers so it wouldn't get infected. Underneath grew a masculine skin. Her cells reconfigured themselves like worker bees around her jaw, her pectorals, her neck, her forearms, and her back, filling up to become hard where before there were just soft curves. It was daybreak when the body, confronted with the total annihilation of the female reproductive system, convulsed again. With contractions that made her lower abdomen rise and fall, she expelled what had been her uterus through her vagina. Her labia sealed in a cellular fizz and quickly formed a scrotum, which would give birth to the testicles, while her clitoris grew, making her stretching skin bleed. Eric removed the old skin as he had done around her nipples, sterilizing as he went along as the makers of Rainbow Brite advised. At noon the next day, Acilde Figueroa was wholly a man. Eric protected his designer body, still encased in raw flesh, with layers of antiseptics and cotton.

The oracle had told Esther Escudero, Omicunlé, that she would receive the Chosen One in her own home, and that she would meet her death at his hands.

Eric sat in a plastic chair next to the bed and battled sleep by contemplating his own death. He thought the scene where death would find him was amusing, and this, his last act of caring for a patient, seemed straight out of the mission statement of the Latin American School of Medicine in Cuba, where he'd graduated. "Science and conscience" was the mantra at the school, which had been founded to create an army of white-robed doctors in service to the most needy, and whose Third World missions the followers of Castro used to excuse everything that had gone wrong with the revolution.

At sunset the Servants of the Apocalypse screamed verses into loudspeakers that the wind blew right into the room: "He had seven stars in his hand, and from his mouth emerged a sharp double-bladed sword." Eric was astonished as he watched the powerful drug accelerate the healing process. The metamorphosis was reaching its conclusion: the skin that would forever protect this masterpiece now covered every altered centimeter of flesh. In contrast to this body's robust health, Eric's was deteriorating. His fragile lungs, already filled with liquid, began to hurt more than he could bear. He'd made a mistake but at least he was on the verge of finishing the job for which he'd been put on earth.

Eric was nine years old when one afternoon, playing marbles in the hallway of his home, his eyes rolled back when he tried to look at his mother, as if he were having an epileptic fit, and he shot out of the house.

They found him on the outskirts of the city, at a ritual in honor of Yemayá, where he had come by himself, speaking in tongues and in Yoruba. That same year, Omidina, who was also the godfather of Esther Escudero, initiated Eric as Babalosha.

In the prophecy delivered at his initiation, it was revealed he would be the one to find Olokun's legitimate son, the one with the seven perfections, the Lord of the Deep. That's why his godfather called him Omioloyu, the Eyes of Yemayá, convinced that one day this clever young boy would discover in the flesh the one who knew what lies at the bottom of the sea.

The oracle had told Esther Escudero, Omicunlé, that she would receive the Chosen One in her own home, and that she would meet her death at his hands. She'd accepted that future calamity with equanimity. She trusted Eric to carry out her plan to have him initiate Omo Olokun when she was no longer here. Eric loved the old woman like a mother and, wanting to avoid the prophecy's fatal outcome, he'd tried to improvise a way out. If he crowned himself as Omo Olokun, he could get rid of Acilde, the supposed Chosen One, but his experiments with the anemone behind Esther's back had ended up making him ill and angering her.

Their evangelical neighbours grew ever more strident. The new Acilde, still dazed, asked Eric what he was doing when he saw him, with a sporadic pulse, writing symbols on the floors and walls. Startled with a sudden fervor, Eric brought the anemone out of the jar. Acilde was still strapped to the bed and asked for a mirror. Eric didn't have time to explain and knelt by the head of the bed, the anemone's tentacles pointing to Acilde's shaved head. Acilde had a crown of moles, dark spots that made a circle all the way around his head. Eric had noticed it when that girl, now finally in the male form she'd so desired, had knelt before him to suck him off that night at the Mirador.

Acting as a priest now, Eric began to pray in a sharp and nasal voice: "Iba Olokun fe mi lo're. Iba Olokun omo re wa se fun oyío." As he prayed, he joined the tentacles to the moles on Acilde's head. A weak Acilde whimpered and cursed, unable to move. The tentacles stayed put, as though with Velcro, and the marine creature's smell hit Eric, the very same stink of garbage from the neighborhood transporting him back to Matanzas Bay, to the sun's silver reflections on the water, a strong smell of iodine and algae that gave the vigor he needed to finish the ritual. "Olokun nuni osi oki elu reye toray. Olokun ni'ka le. Moyugba, Aché." He let go of the creature and brought his face next to Acilde's. "Olokun, here is your child, Eric Vitier, Omioloyu, Omo Yemayá, Okana Di en si Awofaka, I laugh and greet the deity while asking for a blessing." He got even closer to the ear of this newborn man and used his last breath to let him know: "Esther knew what was going to happen. I'm done for. We gave you the body you wanted and now you've given us the body we needed."

ארוחת ערב עם יואכים

הֵד ראשון

SHARRON HASS, born in 1966, is a poet, essayist, and lecturer. Complex, both formally and philosophically, her poetry draws on Hellenistic philosophy and Greek myth to examine the human condition as manifest in a contemporary Israeli context.

שׁוּב רָאִיתִי, אֲנִי הַנִּדּוֹנָה לִרְאִיָּה, לִמְסִירַת
הָאָטוֹם הַבּוֹעֵר שֶׁל הַהֹוֶה עַל הֵדָיו הַשְּׁקוּפִים
חֹמֶר הַנִּפְתָּח לְחֹסֶר הֲבָנוֹת
אֲבָל גַּם לְאֹשֶׁר הַמַּלְכוּת שֶׁל הַנְּתִינָה -

עֵצִים נָפְלוּ מְטוֹסִים חָגוּ הַחֲתוּלָה נָפְלָה קָרְבָּן לְרַעַל
עַכְבָּרִים וּבְטַבּוּרָהּ שֶׁל עִיר הַתְּרוֹמְמָה
הַקָּתֶדְרָלָה שֶׁל הַמִּשְׁפָּחָה הַקְּדוֹשָׁה - מִבַּחוּץ אַרְמוֹן שֶׁל בֹּץ
שֶׁמֶשׁ לֹא תּוּכַל לְהָאִיר, לְבָאֵר; וּמִבִּפְנִים, כְּמוֹ שֶׁגּוּף, גּוּפֵנוּ רָאוּי לוֹ לִהְיוֹת
שְׁטוּף חַרְצִיּוֹת צְהֻבּוֹת מְעוֹפְפוֹת עַל פְּגוּמִים - חֹם וְיֹבֶשׁ מְעוֹרְרֵי הִשְׁתָּאוּת

קָשֶׁה לְהַגִּיעַ אֶל הָרֶגַע הַתָּלוּי מֵעָלַי מֻפְשָׁט וּמְמֹרָק כְּמַרְאָה - מַיִם עוֹמְדִים
סְתוֹרִיִּים בְּשֶׁל אֹבֶךְ זִכְרוֹנוֹת שֶׁלֹּא מוֹתִיר טַחַב אוֹ שְׂרִיטוֹת -
הָאֲפֵלָה זוֹהֶרֶת וְרֵיקָה, נְכוֹנָה לַכֹּל, מְעוֹרֶרֶת פַּחַד חַסְרַת הַפַּחַד

Dinner with Joachim

Translated by
MARCELA SULAK

First Echo

Again I saw, I who am doomed to see, the burning atom
            of the present transmitted on transparent echoes,
                        matter that is open to misunderstanding
but also to the imperial bliss of the giving—

Trees were falling, planes were circling, and the cat was falling prey
            to the rat poison, and in the heart of the city, La Sagrada Familia
                        Cathedral was rising up—from the outside a palace of mud
                                    the sun couldn't illuminate, and inside, like a body, as our bodies should be,
flooded with yellow daisies, flying over scaffolding—heat and dryness that astonish.

            Hard to reach the abstract moment suspended above me burnished as a mirror—still water
            mysterious for the haze of memories that leaves no mold or scratches;
            darkness, shimmer, and emptiness ready for anything, fearlessness inciting fear.

רָאִיתִי רֶגַע בַּעֲבָרוֹ שֶׁל זָה, יְפֵה תֹּאַר הַמְאָרֵחַ שֶׁלִּי בְּרֹאשׁ הַשֻּׁלְחָן
חָתוּל בָּר גָּמִישׁ מָהִיר וְעוֹבֵד אֱלֹהִים אֲחֵרִים,
צוֹחֲקִים לַפְּסִילִים שֶׁאֲנִי קוֹבֶרֶת מִדֵּי יוֹם בְּיוֹמוֹ בָּאוֹר
הָעוֹבֵר מִתַּחַת דֶּלֶת חֲלוֹמוֹתַי   הִגִּישׁ לִי יַיִן וְתוּת וְחַסָּה נוֹצֶצֶת, מוּזָרָה וְעֵרָה
כְּכָל הֶעָלִים הַיְּרֻקִּים שֶׁנִּמְתָּחִים בַּשָּׂדוֹת אֶל הַשֶּׁמֶשׁ, וַחֲבֵרוֹ הַזָּקֵן בִּמְעִיל רַחֲצָה
מוֹסִיף וּמוֹזֵג וּמְדַבֵּר עַל חַיָּיו חַיֵּיהֶם בִּמְדִינוֹת רְחוֹקוֹת שְׁטוּפוֹת רֶצַח יַהֲלוֹמִים בָּתֵּי מִשְׁפָּט
וַאֲהָבוֹת, כְּמוֹ מִטַּלְטְלִין, נִשָּׂאוֹת בִּזְהִירוּת מִמָּקוֹם לְמָקוֹם רְפוּדוֹת נוֹצוֹת
תְּלוּשׁוֹת תַּחֲנוּנִים וּשְׁנֵי אִיּוּמִים...

מָתַי מַקְדִּיחָה סְעוּדָה? הָרֶגַע בּוֹ פֶּשַׁע חוֹבֵר לְשֶׁפַע וּמוֹתִיר אוֹתָנוּ עֲקוּדִים
לִרְאִיָּה מִתְגַּלְגֶּלֶת הָלְאָה וְהָלְאָה בְּמוֹרָדוֹת שֶׁל זְמַן וּמִשְׁפָּחָה קַלָּה שֶׁרַק
שִׁירָה יְכוֹלָה לְלַוּוֹת עַד שֶׁשְּׁאֵרִיּוֹת מוּזִיקָלִיּוֹת שֶׁהִקִּיפוּ כְּבָרָק דָּם לְיַיִן וְכוּ'
תִּתְהַפֵּכְנָה לַפְּעִימָה הַגְּדוֹלָה שֶׁל הָאֹשֶׁר

"אֲנִי כָּאן וַאֲנִי נִפְרָד מִכֶּם" -

I saw a moment in a stranger's past, my beautiful host sitting at the head of the table,
    a quick, lithe wildcat worshipping other gods
        which laugh at the idols I bury each day in the light
        that passes beneath the door of my dreams. He served me wine and strawberries
                and shining lettuce, strange and awake
like all the green field leaves that reach for the sun, and his companion, an old man in a bathrobe,
    continues to pour and speak of his life, their life in far away lands
        flooded with murder, diamonds, courts
            and loves, which, like the furnishings carefully carried from place to place,
                cushioned with feathers, are ripped with pleas and two threats...

When is a meal ruined? At the moment foulness joins fullness and leaves us bound
    to a sight that keeps rolling down the slopes of time and family, a chorus that only
        poetry can accompany until the musical leftovers (lightning, blood to wine, etc.)
        roll themselves into the great beat of happiness

"I'm here, and I take leave of you"—

מָתַי קָם וְהָלַךְ וְרָאִיתִי אוֹתוֹ בַּשֵּׁנִית לוֹחֵץ אֶת יָדִי בַּדֶּלֶת? זְמַן מָה אַחֲרֵי שֶׁחֲבֵרוֹ סִפֵּר
אַחֲרֵי שֶׁסִּפֵּר עַל נְבוּאָה שֶׁיָּרְדָה מֵהֶהָרִים לִקְטֹל אֶת כָּל הַגְּבָרִים אוֹהֲבֵי הַגְּבָרִים וּלְאַחַר שֶׁסִּפֵּר
מְהַדֵּק סְבִיבוֹ אֶת חֲלוּק הָרַחֲצָה כְּחֹל קְטִיפָה הַשּׁוֹמֶרֶת מִכָּל רַע
עַל קוֹנְטֶסוֹת יְשִׁישׁוֹת שֶׁבְּמוֹתָן סוֹחֲרֵי הַפִּשְׁפְּשִׁים קָנוּ רָהִיטִים בְּנֵי מֵאוֹת
בְּמֵאוֹת בּוֹדְדוֹת שֶׁל כֶּסֶף,

בַּמִּרְצָפוֹת נוֹתְרוּ הָאֲבָנִים
עֲלֵיהֶן קוֹפְצוֹת הָאַיָּלוֹת וְהַחֵץ בִּמְעוּפוֹ
לֹא מַשִּׂיג דָּבָר פְּרָט לִמְהִירֻיּוֹת הַמִּסְדְּרוֹן
וְהַנִּבְרָשׁוֹת הַנּוֹצְצוֹת מֵעַל מְהִירוּתוֹ

אַחֲרֵי שֶׁחֲבֵרוֹ סִפֵּר קָם חֶרֶשׁ יְהוֹיָכִים וְסָגַר אַחֲרָיו אֶת דֶּלֶת חֲדַר הַמְּשָׁרְתִים
בַּמִּסְדְּרוֹן -
אֵי שָׁם בְּיַלְדוּתוֹ ... הַמִּדְבָּר הַיָּרֹק ...
אָבִיו קָשַׁר אוֹתוֹ בַּחֲבָלִים   וְהֵנִיף

When did he get up and go, and I see him once more pressing my hand at the door? Some time
after his companion told,
after he told of the prophecy that went down from the mountains to slay all the men who love men,
and after he told,
wrapping himself in his blue velvet bathrobe that protects him from all evil,
about the old countesses from whom, upon their death, the flea market merchant bought
century's old furniture for hundreds of silver coins.

In the floor tiles there were stones
over which does were leaping; the arrow in its flight
never reaches anything but the swiftness of a corridor
and the chandeliers that are shining above that swiftness.

After his companion told, he got up silently and closed the servant's door behind him
in the corridor—
somewhere in his childhood...the green desert...
his father tied him in ropes   and raised
him naked to a hook   secured in a crossbeam whipping him for hours on end
swinging (there was some reason, a reason like an echo rising from misunderstandings,

עֵירֹם לְטַבַּעַת   מֻשְׁחָל לְקֶשֶׁת צוֹלֶבֶת צוֹלֵף בּוֹ שָׁעוֹת אֲרֻכּוֹת
מִתְנַדְנֵד   (הָיְתָה אֵיזוֹ סִבָּה, סִבָּה כְּמוֹ הֵד קְשׁוּרָה בְּחֹסֶר הַהֲבָנוֹת הַמִּתְפַּשְּׁטוֹת
אוּלַי שִׂחֵק בְּבֻבּוֹת אוּלַי הָאָב רָצָה לְשׂוֹחֵחַ עִם אֱלֹהֵי הַזַּעַם הַשָּׁחֹר הַנּוֹרָא
שֶׁהָיָה תּוֹקֵף בְּאַחַת מֵהַשַּׁבָּתוֹת חַסְרוֹת הַשּׁוּלַיִם שֶׁאַלְכּוֹהוֹל הֶעֱנִיק לָהֶן כְּמֵעֵין
אִמְרָה מְזַמֶּרֶת עֲמוּמָה עַל חַיִּים אֲחֵרִים)

אֶלֶף זְרוֹעוֹת פּוֹשְׁטִים הָאֵלִים לִקְרָאתֵנוּ פְּעוּרֵי פֶּה
מִי עָבַר בֶּחָרָבָה? מִי נִשְׁאַר עַל גָּדָה? מִי הִבִּיט לְאָחוֹר וּמִי
אָפֹר מִמַּיִם וָאֵשׁ? לֹא אֲנִי הַיּוֹדֵעַ וְגַם לֹא אֶת הָרַע רָאִיתִי
אֶת הַתַּאֲוָה לְסַחֵר בֵּין דָּם לְיַיִן - מְאַהֵב זָקֵן מְכַרְבֵּל יַהֲלוֹמִים
נָהַג בִּי כְּמוֹ הָיִיתִי אֵל וְנָתַן לִי לֶאֱכֹל חֲתִיכַת אָדָם
אוּלַי כָּךְ רוֹצִים לְהִפָּרֵד לְשָׁלוֹם מִבְּלִי לוֹמַר אֶת מִלּוֹת הַפְּרִידָה
וּמַעֲנִיקִים מַה שֶּׁלְּאַחֲרָיו תּוּכַל רַק הַשִּׁירָה לְלַווֹת -
כַּפָּרָה מִתְמֶדֶת עַל הָעַיִן הַפְּקוּחָה

מֵעַל הַשֻּׁלְחָן שֶׁיּוֹשְׁבָיו הִתְפַּזְּרוּ לְכָל הָרוּחוֹת
הֵדֵי הַצְּחוֹק הַסַּכִּין הַדֶּלֶת הַנִּסְגֶּרֶת
קִפְלֵי אוֹר הָרֶגַע הַזֶּה הַלֹּא נִכְנָע, הַמִּתְפַּצֵּל, הַבּוֹעֵר,
הַמְיֻעָד לִמְסִירָה

perhaps he played with dolls, perhaps his father would speak with the gods of the awful
black anger that hit him one of those marginless Sabbaths and which alcohol endowed
with a kind of obscure edge humming of other lives).

The gods are stretching a thousand arms toward us, who stand agape.
        Who crossed on dry land, who was left on the shore, who was looking back, and who
is gray with water and fire? I am not one to know, and I didn't see evil
but the lust for commerce between blood and wine—and an old lover wrapped with diamonds
        treated me as if I were a god and gave me to eat a piece of a man;
        maybe this is the way one wants to say goodbye without saying the words of parting,
and one gives that which, afterward, only poetry can accompany—
                                        the constant atonement of the open eye,

echoes of laughter from the guests at the table
spread to the four winds, over the knife, the closing door,
the folds of light, this moment that is unrelenting, that is splitting, that is burning,
that is meant to be given.

הֵד שני

זֶהוּ טִיּוּלָם שֶׁל הַדּוֹמְמִים בְּאֶרֶץ הַפְּלָאוֹת

כִּתְרֵי קַשְׁתוֹת הָאֶבֶן הִתְרוֹמְמוּ לְהַכְתִּירָם

בָּאוֹר הָיָה הַשַּׁיִשׁ מוֹצִיא עָלִים וּמְלַבְלֵב

וּפְגוּמִים עֲלֵיהֶם תְּלוּיִים בַּנָּאִים עֲשָׂרוֹת שָׁנִים

מְיַחֲלִים לְמִגְדָּל נוֹסָף לְשִׁכְבַת הָאֲוִיר שֶׁתְּבוֹדֵד

נִכְסָפִים לְתַלְוּלִיּוֹת מִפְּשָׁט מְקֻטָּעוֹת כָּךְ שֶׁהֶעָקֹם

וְהַמִּקְרִי יִפָּגְשׁוּ בַּמְעֻקָּל וּבַמְקֻמָּר – בִּרְמִיזָה

שֶׁהַהִתְמַסְּרוּת אֵלֶיהָ לֹא כְּרוּכָה בְּאָבְדָן וּבְאָסוֹן

Second Echo

This is the tour of the silent in the wonderland of Barcelona

The crowns of the stone arches were raised to crown them

The marble blossoms and opens its leaves in the light

And the scaffolds on which the builders have been hanging for decades

Yearn for another tower, a layer of insulating air

Long for piles of fragmented abstractions so the crooked

And the coincidental will meet with the curves and the arches—hinting

That its devotions are not bound to loss and disaster

Translated by Marcela Sulak • Hebrew | Israel

כָּזוֹ אַרְכִיטֶקְטוּרָה פָּגְשׁוּ הַדּוֹמְמִים מֵעֶלְבּוֹן

הוֹ אֱלֹהִים אֲנִי כּוֹתֶבֶת בְּתוֹךְ קִרְעֵי נְיָר

וְאָבָק וְרֶשֶׁת חוּטִים בִּלְתִּי נִפְרָמִים

שֶׁל יוֹמְיוֹם: מֵעָלֵינוּ הַנּוֹסְעִים הִתְרוֹמְמָה קָתֶדְרָלָה שֶׁל חַרְצִיּוֹת אֶבֶן

אִישׁ אֶחָד הֶעֱנִיק לְעִיר אַחַת מַתְּנַת בְּנִיָּה בִּלְתִּי פּוֹסֶקֶת

לְכַפֵּר עַל חֲטָאִים (לֹא יְדוּעִים לִי) שֶׁל אַנְשֵׁי הָעִיר

כָּךְ עַל גּוּפֵנוּ לְהֵרָאוֹת מִבִּפְנִים בִּזְמַן הַתֹּם אוֹ הַחֶמְלָה

הַמִּתְפַּשְּׁטִים כָּעֲיֵפוּת הַמְּתוּקָה בְּגוּפָם שֶׁל הָעֲיֵפִים שֶׁעוֹבְרִים מֵאֵין אוֹנִים

חֹסֶר הַשֵּׁנָה שֶׁל נְדוּדֵי הַמְּתָשִׁים הַלְּבָנִים אֶל הַשֵּׁנָה

הָעֲמֻקָּה שֶׁל הַצַּדִּיקִים לְלַיְלָה - אֵלּוּ הַמַּבְרִיאִים לְלֹא חֲלוֹמוֹת

Such was the architecture met by the ones silenced by insult

Oh God, I'm writing in the midst of paper shreds

And dust and a net of tangled threads

Of the quotidian: Above us, the travelers, the cathedral of stone daisies rises

One person has given to one city a gift of unending construction

To atone for the sins (unknown to me) of the city's inhabitants

This is how our bodies should look from the inside in the moment of compassion

That spreads like sweet fatigue in the bodies of the weary that pass from

The pale, sleeplessness of the tossed and turned

Into the sleep of the saints for one night—the ones that convalesce without dreaming

כָּךְ עוֹמֶדֶת הַקָּתֶדְרָלָה בְּאֶמְצָעָהּ שֶׁל עִיר - נֹגַהּ הַהִתְעוֹרְרוּת לְחַיִּים

לְלֹא הַצַּעַר שֶׁל הַמָּוֶת שֶׁמּוֹסִיף לְסַלֵּק מֵעַל פָּנֵינוּ כָּל שִׂמְחָה קְטַנָּה

כְּעֶלְבּוֹן לַגְּדֻלָּה שֶׁהָיְתָה מְקִיצָה אוֹתָנוּ לַחַיִּים אוּלַי הָיוּ אֵלּוּ חַרְצִיּוֹת הָאוֹר הַנִּפְקָחוֹת

כְּתָרִים לְשׁוּמְאִישׁ שֶׁאֵין צֹרֶךְ בָּהֶם לֹא לְאֵל אֶחָד גָּדוֹל מִזְדַּקֵּן וְלֹא לְאַחֵר תָּלוּי עַל עֵץ

כְּתָרִים שֶׁל חַרְצִיּוֹת הָאוֹר הַחַי הַצָּהֹב, הַלָּבָן, הָרוֹטֵט גְּשׁוּשִׁים וְנִמְשָׁךְ כְּתַבְנִית גְּדוֹלָה

לֹא-מְנֻפֶּצֶת שֶׁל רְשָׁתוֹת וּמְנִיפוֹת וְנַחֲשֵׁי הַגִּידִים הַבּוֹעֲרִים מִתְנוּפָה

לָנוּ, לָאֱנוֹשִׁי, תָּלָה הָאֱנוֹשִׁי בְּגֹבַהּ הַמֵּאִיר מִסְתּוֹר   אָנָלוֹגְיָה לִצְמֹחַ בָּהּ

עַד שֶׁאֶתְעַצֵּם לְגַמְרֵי לְמִדּוֹתַי שֶׁהֵן לֹא יוֹתֵר מֵהַמֶּטֶר שִׁשִּׁים וְאֶרְאֶה וְאֶהְיֶה כְּלוּלָה בָּרְאִי

So stands the cathedral in the city's center—the radiance of waking to life

Without the remorse of death that removes from us every small joy

As an insult to the great joy that was awakening us to life, perhaps, the light's chrysanthemums opening

Crowning the no-man, there is no need for them, for the one, great, aging God, not the one hanging on the tree

Unshattered form of nets and fans and serpentine tendons, burning tendons, burning from their momentum

To us, to the humane, the human hanging in their shining heights, a secret shelter, and analogy growing within it

Until I grow totally into myself, to my full measure that is not more than a meter sixty, then I will see and I will be gathered into the seeing

הֵד שלישי

יָשַׁבְנוּ חֲמִשָּׁה לַשֻּׁלְחָן - זוּג גְּבָרִים, זוּג נָשִׁים וּמְשָׁרֶתֶת אַחַת, אֶלִיזַבֶּת
מֵעַל רָאשֵׁינוּ זָרְחוּ נִבְרְשׁוֹת אוֹסְטְרִיּוֹת וְלוּלָאָה אַחַת נֶעֶלְמָה בָּהּ כָּל אֶחָד רָצָה
לִתְפֹּס דַּג זָהָב שֶׁזִּנֵּק מִמִּשְׁאָלָה שֶׁחָזַרְנוּ עָלֶיהָ פְּעָמִים רַבּוֹת
עַד לְאֵין אוֹנִים וּבוּשָׁה - הַמִּשְׁאָלָה כְּמוֹ צְלָב שָׁחֹר אוֹ חֲטוֹטֶרֶת
אוּלַי הַיּוֹם אוּלַי עַכְשָׁו בַּאֲרוּחַת הָעֶרֶב יְזַנֵּק הַדָּג זָהָב וְיַעֲנִיק לָנוּ אֶת הַמִּשְׁאָלָה
הַסּוֹתֶרֶת לַמִּשְׁאָלָה שֶׁהָפְכָה מִמַּיִם חַיִּים לְמַרְאָה חַסְרַת פַּחַד - צָלוּל וְעֵר הַמָּקוֹם הָרֵיק

לַמְשָׁרֶתֶת יֵשׁ שֵׁם, נִקְרְאָה לְלֹא הֶרֶף לְהוֹרִיד וּלְהַעֲלוֹת
וּבְיָשְׁבָהּ בֵּינֵינוּ הִקְטִינָה עַצְמָהּ הִגְדִּילָה עַצְמָהּ בְּשִׂיחָה בְּשָׂפָה הַזָּרָה לִשְׂפָתָהּ
אָכְלָה בְּעֵינַיִם פְּקוּחוֹת גְּבִינָה וּבְעֵינַיִם פְּקוּחוֹת שָׁתְתָה שַׁמְפַּנְיָה וְלֹא הָיָה לָהּ הַלּוּקְסוּס
שֶׁל אֲדוֹנִים וּגְבִירוֹת לְמַצְמֵץ וְלִבְהוֹת - וְנֶעֶלְמָה מֵאֲחוֹרֵי דֶּלֶת אַחַת בְּמִסְדְּרוֹן אָרֹךְ
שָׁם בְּפְסֵיפַס הָרְצָפוֹת חֵץ רוֹדֵף אַחֲרֵי אַיָּלָה כּוֹכָבִים זוֹרְחִים לְיַד חֲדַר הַשֵּׁנָה וְהַשֶּׁמֶשׁ

Third Echo

We five sat at the table—male couple, female couple, and one maid, Elizabeth
    Over our heads the Austrian chandelier with one loop missing glowed, each one wanted
to catch the golden fish that leaps from the wish we've returned to so many times
until the wish is helpless and embarrassed, like a black crucifix or a hump
    Maybe today, maybe now at this evening's meal, the golden fish will leap to grant us the
        wish
that contradicts the wish that turned life from the waters to the looking glass, in simple
  balance—clear and conscious of the empty place

The maid has a name, she was constantly summoned to lower and to raise
    She sat down to make herself smaller in our eyes but larger in our conversation in a
        language foreign to her lips
She ate with eyes open on the garden and drank with eyes open, champagne, not having the luxury
of lords and ladies to blink and to stare—she disappeared through the door down a long corridor
    There in the flooring mosaic an arrow in pursuit of a doe

עוֹלָה בְּקִרְבַת הַסָּלוֹן

נוֹתַרְנוּ אַרְבָּעָה זָרִים - שְׁנַיִם מוּל שְׁנַיִם בִּמְהִירֻיּוֹת שׁוֹנוֹת הֶחְלַפְנוּ לְלֹא תְּנוּעָה
כִּסְאוֹת וְנֶאֱמָנֻיּוֹת וּכְשֶׁהַלַּיְלָה גָּבַר וְהָאַלְכּוֹהוֹל הֶעֱמִיק אֶת הַגְּבוּל הַצַּר בֵּין צִפִּיָּה
לְבָאוֹת כְּמוֹ קְדוֹשִׁים שֶׁמֵּעֲלֵיהֶם מְרַחֶפֶת הִלָּה זוֹרַחַת הָפַכְנוּ גַּם אֲנַחְנוּ
מְקֻטָּעִים וּטְרוּפֵי וִדּוּי - מַה יִּהְיֶה הָרֶגַע הַנָּכוֹן לָקוּם וְלוֹמַר תּוֹדָה וְשָׁלוֹם
בְּמָקוֹם נוֹסָף מִבֵּין הַמְּקוֹמוֹת בָּהֶם הָאִינְטִימִי נִתָּן לְלֹא גְּבוּל כִּי נִתָּן לְמִי
שֶׁהוּא עַד חִנָּם, זֶה שֶׁלֹּא יֵדַע שֶׁסּוֹד הוּא סוֹד שֶׁלְּרֹאשׁוֹ לוּלָאָה וְלֹא רֶשֶׁת
וְאֵין בּוֹ כְּדֵי לְהַזִּיק - נְדִיבוּת קַלָּה שֶׁל אוֹרְחִים לְלַיְלָה אֶחָד שֶׁאֵינָם רוֹצִים לֶאֱחֹז
וּבְהַכָּרַת הַתּוֹדָה מְהוּלָה כְּבָר הַשִּׁכְחָה הַטּוֹבָה

וְאָז נָהֲגוּ בָּנוּ כְּמוֹ הָיִינוּ אֵלִים, לֹא קְדוֹשִׁים חַסְרֵי כֹּל עַל מִפְתַּן הַזֹּהַר, כְּמוֹ אֵלִים
רְעֵבִים שֶׁאֵין לָדַעַת מַה יַּשְׂבִּיעֵם וּמַה יָּקִים אוֹתָם מֵהַשֻּׁלְחָן אֶל הַדֶּלֶת
בְּטֶרֶם הִבְחַנּוּ כְּבָר הָיָה פִּינוּ מָלֵא בַּפֶּצַע שֶׁהֻגַּשׁ לְחִכֵּנוּ, בִּילִי עָטוּף קְטִיפַת עַד
כְּחֻלָּה אָמַרְתָּ אַתָּה מַסְכִּים יְהוֹיָכִים שֶׁאֲסַפֵּר וִיהוֹיָכִים הֶחָלָק כַּחֲתוּל בָּר וְזָרִיז
מִיֹּפִי שֶׁאֵין בּוֹ תָּוִים רְמוּסִים כֻּלּוֹ הַסּוּס וְנִימוּס מָשַׁךְ בִּכְתֵפָיו "סַפֵּר" וּמְזָרִים
הָפַכְנוּ לְדֶמֶטֶר אוֹ זֶאוּס לוֹעֲסִים בְּשַׂר אֱנוֹשִׁי וְחַי - מְקַלְּלִים אֶת הָרֶגַע בּוֹ הַסַּכִּין
הֶחֱלִיקָה בֵּין קִפְלֵי הַשֶּׁפַע וּמָצְאָה אֶת הַקָּשֶׁה וְהַסָּמוּי בָּרֹךְ חֲסַר הַפָּנִים שֶׁל הַפְּרִי

stars shining next to the bedroom and the sun
    rising near the salon

We remained, four strangers—two facing two, without moving, we changed seats and allegiances
with varying speeds, and when the night strengthened and the alcohol deepened the narrow border
    between expectation and what was to come, and like the shining haloed saints floating
    above, we also broke, frenzied with confessions—what is the right time to rise, say thank
you and goodbye, from a place where intimacy knows no bounds, since it is given to someone
still free, who doesn't know that this secret is a secret; over his head is a slipknot not a net,
and no harm will come—a guest's easy generosity, is that they want just a night, not forever,
    and the gratitude is already mixed with a kind forgetfulness

And we were treated like gods, not like pauper saints on the threshold of radiance, but like gods
    so hungry you don't know what to give them to sate them, what will make them leave the
        table and head to the door,
    before we noticed, our mouths were filled with the wound we had been served, Billy
        wrapped in eternal
blue velvet, said, do you permit me to tell? Joachim, sleek as a wild cat, swift with beauty
and unblemished features, hesitantly, politely shrugged his shoulders, "tell." And from strangers,

אֶת הַכֹּל יֵשׁ לְלַוּוֹת בְּשִׁירָה וּמוּזִיקָה – בְּיַלְדוּתוֹ
נִתְלָה בִּידֵי אָבִיו עֵירֹם וְקָשׁוּר עַל טַבַּעַת בַּרְזֶל שְׁקוּעָה
בַּתִּקְרָה, צָף שָׁעוֹת מְפַרְפֵּר בָּאֲוִיר וּמְצַלֵּף לָמָּה
וּמַדּוּעַ אֵינֶנּוּ יוֹדְעִים לְעוֹלָם לֹא נֵדַע וּמַה חֲשׁוּבָה סִבָּה אַחַת
מֵאֶלֶף אֲחֵרוֹת פְּזוּרוֹת כָּמוֹהָ בֶּעָבָר - דַּרְכֵּנוּ אֶל הָרֶגַע, אֶל הָאֹשֶׁר
אֶל הַהֹוֶה חֲסַר הַתֹּכֶן כִּי פְּנֵי הַחֲלוֹם וּפְנֵי הַיּוֹם הֵם בְּגֹבַהּ הַמַּיִם, הַמַּרְאוֹת
הָרוֹעֲדוֹת וְהָרֵיקוֹת - קְלָלָה אֲרֻכָּה הִטִּילוּ הָאֵלִים בַּמְּאָרְחִים בְּצֶאֱצָאֵי יַלְדֵי הַיְלָדִים
וְלֹא חָזְרוּ לָשֶׁבֶת לַשֻּׁלְחָנוֹת הָעֲרוּכִים, לַכִּסֵּא הָרֵיק, לַפִּתּוּיִים בֵּין הַיַּיִן לַדָּם -
זְרוֹעוֹתֵיהֶם פְּשׁוּטוֹת אֵלֵינוּ, וְהַחֲבָלִים מְתוּחִים, וְהָרְשָׁתוֹת פְּרוּשׂוֹת, וְהַקָּרְבָּן מֻגָּשׁ
שֶׁלֹּא בַּשָּׁעָה הַיְעוּדָה וּמַחֲמִיץ, שׁוּב מַחְמִיץ אֶת הַמִּשְׁאָלָה הַנְּכוֹנָה אוֹ הַמִּלָּה
יְהוֹיָכִים קָם וְנֶעֱלַם, גַּם אֲנַחְנוּ קַמְנוּ וְנֶעֱלַמְנוּ בַּפֶּתַח הַגָּבוֹהַּ, זֶה הָעוֹמֵד בֵּין הַשֶּׁמֶשׁ
לַכּוֹכָבִים, שִׁכּוֹרוֹת בְּמִסְדְּרוֹן-הַסַּחַר-בֵּין-הַנְּשָׁמוֹת

we became Demeter and Zeus, munching on human meat—cursing the moment the knife
slides into the wrinkle of aplenty and hits upon the pit hidden in the faceless softness of fruit

Everything should be accompanied by music and singing—in his childhood
he was hanged by his father, naked, and tied to an iron ring suspended from the ceiling,
twitching for hours in the air and whipped, why,
we don't know, we'll never know, and what does it matter, one reason
from the thousand others scattered in the past—our path to the moment, to happiness,
to a present lacking substance—because the face of the dream and the face of the day are
empty mirrors quivering—the gods cursed the hosts and the descendents of their children,
and they didn't return to the set tables, the empty chair, to the temptations of blood and wine—
the arms of the gods are stretching to us, the ropes are tight, the nets are spread, but the
sacrifice given
at the wrong hour, has spoiled, and again the wish expires or the word
Joachim rose and disappeared, we, too, rose and disappeared in arched entrance, the one that stood
between the sun and the stars, drunk in the corridor where the souls traffic

הֵד רביעי

זֶה אוֹרָהּ שֶׁל הַנֶּפֶשׁ: תְּכֵלֶת קָרָה וַעֲרָפֶל

סְלִילִים כְּמוֹ עָשָׁן עוֹלִים מִבֵּית הַקּוֹנְכִיָּה

וְעִם הַלֹּבֶן הַנִּשְׁטָף, הַנִּרְאֶה, מִתְרוֹמֶמֶת

שׁוּב, הַשְּׁאֵלָה, הַפִּגּוּם, הַסְּפִּירָלָה שֶׁל הָאֶבֶן

הַפְּתוּחָה, זוֹ הַמְכַסָּה עַכְשָׁו עַל הֶעְדֵּר, מִי בֵּיתוֹ שֶׁל מִי

הַגּוּף הַזֶּה הַפָּעוּר לְרוּחַ וּמִקְרֶה, אוֹ הַנֶּפֶשׁ הַמְנַסָּה

לַחֲמֹק מִלְּפִיתַת מַעְגָּלִים. אוֹ אוּלַי אַחֶרֶת לְגַמְרֵי, הַמָּקוֹם הַזֶּה,

מִבִּפְנִים עָשָׂה אוֹתוֹ בּוֹנֵה הַקּוֹנְכִיּוֹת, מְגַשֵּׁשׁ דֶּרֶךְ לַצּוּרָה

Fourth Echo

This is the light of the soul: cold azure and fog

Coils like smoke arising from the house of the conch

And with the rinsed, visible whiteness, the question

Rises again, the scaffolding and the open spire of

Stone, that now covers the absence, who is the home of whom?

Is it this body, exposed to wind and to chance, or the soul which

Tries to escape from the grasp of circles. In other words, this place

Was built by the builder of conchs from within, groping a way to a form

הַמַּשִׁיקָה לַחֶזְיוֹנוֹת, כִּי יִתָּכֵן וְהַדָּבָר שֶׁהוּא מְקֻפָּל בּוֹ, הוּא מְקַפֵּל אוֹתוֹ בְּתוֹכוֹ,

וְהַדָּבָר הוּא גַּם הֶחָלָל, הוֹלֵךְ וְגָדֵל, וְהוֹלֵךְ וְקָטֵן, כִּבְצָלִים, טֶלֶסְקוֹפּ, אוֹ בֻּבַּת הַבַּבּוּשְׁקָה

אֲבָל גַּם אוֹר הַנֹּהַר כְּמִקַּרְקָעִית הֲפוּכָה שֶׁל עָפָר פּוֹרֵץ וּמַבְקִיעַ עַד לַמּוֹלֶקוּלָה הָאַחֲרוֹנָה

עַד הָרְפָאִים הַתְּכֻלִּים שֶׁהֵם אָח לְשֶׁמֶשׁ גָּדוֹל וְצָהֹב, וּבְתָוֶךְ הַפְּעִירָה, בֵּין הַכָּחֹל לַצָּהֹב

הַפְּעִירָה, בֵּיתוֹ שֶׁל עוֹשֵׂה צוּרוֹת שְׁטוּפוֹת יָם וְחוֹל, צוּרוֹת שְׁטוּפוֹת זְמַן וְנוֹהֲמוֹת

זֶה אוֹרָהּ שֶׁל הַנֶּפֶשׁ - הָאוֹר הָעוֹלֶה מֵהָעֹמֶק טֶרֶם קְרִיסָה - מַה שֶּׁמָּתוּחַ בֵּין קְטָבִים, וּמְצַפֶּה,

הַקּוֹלוֹת שֶׁעוֹלִים, קוֹלוֹת הַהוּרִיקָן וְהַבֶּהָלָה, סוֹלְלִים שְׁבִיל בִּבְלְתִּי נִרְאֶה שָׁם הַמְּדוּזָה מְחַלֶּפֶת

That will graze visions because maybe that in which he is enveloped, he is enveloping it in
himself

And that thing is space, growing and shrinking like onions, telescopes, and matryoshka dolls

But also a light radiating as from the depths of the earth, bursting and breaking to the last molecule

To those blue specters that are brothers to a big yellow sun, and in the middle, the opening
between the blue and the yellow

The opening, the house of the builder, of forms rinsed with sea and sand, forms rinsed with time
and with roaring

This is the light of the soul—the light that rises from the deep before collapsing—that which is tied
between the poles, and waiting

The voices that rise, voices of hurricane and fear, paving a path in the invisible, there the medusa is
replaced

בְּרַעַשׁ גָּדוֹל בֵּין צְמָחִים נִשְׁבָּרִים בִּיצוּר שְׁמֵימִי, עָסוּק וְנִרְגָּז, מְעֻטָּר נוֹצוֹת וְעָלִים, זֶה הַמּוּזִי פּוֹתֵחַ
הַשְּׁעָרִים (רוֹצֶה
  לֹא רוֹצֶה לֶאֱחֹז)
הַמַּמְשִׁיךְ לְהִתְפַּתֵּל בַּחֹשֶׁךְ, כִּי אֵי שָׁם בֵּין סְלִילִים תְּלוּיִים הַכּוֹכָבִים, מַקְהֵלוֹת שֶׁשָּׁרוֹת לְלֹא ;גִּבּוֹר
זֶהוּ אוֹרָהּ הַמִּתְהַפֵּךְ שֶׁל הַנֶּפֶשׁ

קֶרַח וַאֲבָנִים רֵיקוֹת, סִימָנֵי חֲרִיכָה שֶׁל אֵשׁ גְּדוֹלָה שֶׁהוֹתִירָה מֵחֲמֵשֶׁת הַחוּשִׁים רַק

אֶת חוּשׁ הָעִוָּרוֹן, זֶה הַזּוֹכֵר מַה מַּשְׁמָעוֹ שֶׁל חֶסֶד, לִרְאוֹת אֲהוּבְךָ הָעֵירֹם
אוֹכֵל אֶת לִבְּךָ מִחוּצָה לְךָ,-

וְכָעֵת אֵין חָלָל לְהַנִּיחַ גּוּף נוֹפֵל   בּוֹעֵר

הָאַהֲבָה – (הַאִם נִתָּן לִטֹּל מֵהָאַסְטְרוֹנוֹם
אֶת הַמַּעְגָּל) - הַאִם הִיא מְקֻפֶּלֶת בָּנוּ אוֹ אֲנַחְנוּ בָּהּ, מְחֲרִיכַת

with a great tumult among broken plants, with divine creature, busy and annoyed, decorated with
    feathers and leaves

This is the muse-like opening gates, (wanting
not wanting to hold)
that continues to wind in the dark,
because somewhere between coils the stars are hanging, choirs that sing without a hero
it is the overturned light of the soul.

Ice and hollow stones, scorch marks of a great fire that left of the five senses, only the sense of
    blindness

The sense that remembers the meaning of grace, which is seeing your naked beloved eating your
    heart removed from your body—

And now there is nowhere to set a falling, burning body

Love—(can we take the circle from the astronomer?)—
is it enveloped in us, or are we enveloped in it, from the scorch

הַקִּפָּאוֹן אֲנִי זוֹכֶרֶת אֶת הַמְּגוּרִים עַל הַשֶּׁמֶשׁ הֵיכָן הָאֵשׁ

וְהַמַּעְגָּל הָיוּ שֵׁמוֹת נִרְדָּפִים לְחֹמֶר (אֲנִי הַחֹמֶר)   לְכוּדָה בָּאוֹר, רָקַדְתִּי אֶת צֶנְטְרִיפוּגוֹת הָאוֹר

of frost I remember living on the sun, where fire and
circle were synonyms for matter (I am the matter)
Trapped in light, I danced the centrifuges of light

הֵד חמישי

הַדָּגִים נָחוּ בְּשׁוּרוֹת עַל קַרְטוֹן זָהָב. מִישֶׁהוּ
רָכַן בֵּינוֹת לַסְּנַפִּירִים אֲבָל רַק לְרֶגַע רַךְ.
הַזָּהָב הַזּוֹל הִסְעִיר מֵחָדָשׁ אֵלִים
עַתִּיקִים, וְנִזְכַּרְנוּ אֵיךְ גַּם אִם חַיֵּינוּ קְשׁוּרִים בְּחַיִּים
אֲחֵרִים רוֹפֶפֶת כָּל כָּךְ לְעִתִּים עַל רֶקַע בּוֹעֵר הַהַבְחָנָה
בֵּין רֶצַח לְמַתָּנָה. וְהִשְׁתַּחֲוָה בֵּינוֹ לְבֵין עַצְמוֹ עַל הַקַּו הַנֶּעֱלָם
שֶׁל הַמַּיִם וְהַנְּשָׁמוֹת, חֲגִיגִי, לְהַרְשׁוֹת לְעַצְמוֹ אֶת הָרָעָב מוּל הַשֶּׁפַע
הַלֶּהָבָה הַבּוֹעֶרֶת בְּתוֹכְכֵי הַיּוֹם.

עַכְשָׁו לַיְלָה, רָחוֹק אַחֲרֵי חֲצוֹת. שׁוּם אִשָּׁה לֹא הוֹתִירָה סַנְדָּל מֵאָחוֹר.
הַצַּלָּחוֹת רֵיקוֹת. הָרְשָׁתוֹת מִתְנַדְנְדוֹת בַּחַלּוֹן. הָאוֹרְחִים שֶׁאֵינָם יוֹדְעִים
לַעֲזֹב בְּשֶׁל עֲיֵפוּת גְּדוֹלָה אוֹ אַהֲבָה לַמְאָרְחִים הַשְּׂרוּעִים ---(אוּלַי עַכְשָׁו תֵּאָמֵר
הַמִּלָּה, מֵאָחוֹר, מֵאֲחוֹרֵי זְמַן הַחֲגִיגוֹת, וְתַצִּית נִסָּיוֹן חַיִּים לִתְוּבָנָה אַחַת וִיחִידָה,
בְּבַיִת שֶׁפָּתַח שְׁעָרָיו וְסָגַר וּפָתַח, כִּלְוְיָתָן אוֹ יַבֶּשֶׁת תַּת יַמִּית אַחֶרֶת
הַמְכַסָּה עָלֵינוּ בְּעוֹד לְמַעְלָה הַסְּעָרוֹת וְהַטְּבִיעָה וְהָאוֹתוֹת הַנִּתָּנִים
לְפַרְשָׁנוּת, לֹא בְּלִי גְּבוּל)

Fifth Echo

The fish rest in rows upon the gold cardboard. Someone
bends over the fins, but only bends for a moment.
The cheap gold stirs the ancient gods
anew. And though we recalled that our lives are linked to other
lives, sometimes the line between murder and gift is so loose when thrown
against a burning background. He bends within himself over the vanishing thread between water
and souls, festive, allowing himself the hunger that precedes
abundance, the flame inside the day.

Now is night, long after midnight. No woman has left a sandal behind,
the plates are empty, nets are swinging in the windows. The guests who don't know
how to leave, from great fatigue, or for love of the recumbent hosts (maybe now the word
will be pronounced behind the time of festivals, now experience combust into a single
thought
in a house that has opened its doors, and closed, and opened, a whale, or another

אֲנִי פּוֹנָה בְּלִבִּי אֶל מִי שֶׁפָּתְחָה לְמַעֲנִי
תַּחְבִּיר וּשְׁבִילִים נְקִיִּים מֵאֵזוֹב בָּאִידְיוֹסִינְקְרָטִי - זוֹ רָמָה, שְׂרוּעָה
כִּמְכַשֵּׁף שֶׁאֵלָיו דִּבְּרוּ דְּגֵי הַזָּהָב בְּעוֹדָם מִתְבַּשְּׁלִים בַּסִּירִים הַגְּדוֹלִים
וּבְקוֹל הַקַּר, הַמַּפְתִּיעַ שֶׁל נְבוּאוֹת הַנֶּפֶשׁ (הַחָכְמָה הַנִּצְבֶּרֶת בְּמָקוֹם שֶׁנּוֹתְרוּ
בּוֹ אוֹ צַעַר אוֹ זִכְרוֹנוֹת) הֵצֵנּוּ אֶת הַלֶּהָבוֹת וְחָזְרוּ אֶל הַיָּם, כָּךְ נוֹתְרָה יָד אַחַת
בָּאֵשׁ הַדּוֹלֶקֶת בַּמִּטְבָּחִים, בַּמַּיִם, בָּאָבָק, בָּעֲיֵפוּת שֶׁאֵין לָהּ דְּמוּת וְצֶלֶם תְּפִלָּה
וְיָד אַחַת בַּחוּטִים הַפְּרוּמִים שֶׁל עֲלִילוֹת בָּהֶן נִלְכֶּדֶת נֶפֶשׁ שֶׁאֵינָהּ יוֹדַעַת לְהַבְדִּיל

עַצְמָהּ בַּפִּצּוּלִים, וְרַק בַּלֵּילוֹת וּלְאַט כָּל כָּךְ אָנוּ פּוֹרְמוֹת אֶת הַקַּיִץ הַזֶּה

לַהֲבָנָה שֶׁהָאֱמֶת בְּסוֹפוֹ שֶׁל דָּבָר לֹא מַמָּשׁ

מְשַׁנָּה.

underwater continent
that covers us, while above, the storms and the drowning and the signs are given
to interpretation not without end).

In my heart I turn to the one who opened for me
syntax and a path through idiosyncrasy clear of moss—it's Rama, my friend, sprawled
like a magician to whom the golden fish spoke while the big pots were boiling,
and in a cold voice, the astonishing prophecies of the soul (the wisdom that accumulates
in the place
where grief or memories are left) cooled the flames and returned to the sea, so one hand
is left in the burning kitchen fire, in the water, in the dust, in the fatigue bereft an image
or idol to pray to
and the other hand is left in the unraveling threads of narratives, in which the soul, which doesn't
know how to distinguish
itself in its forkings, is caught; only in the night, and slowly, we unravel this summer
to an understanding that the truth of it doesn't actually matter.

הֵד שִׁישִׁי

מַלְאָךְ עַל מִפְתַּן הַחֶדֶר מִדֵּי יוֹם מְצַפֶּה לִקְרִיאָה

אֶל הָרַחֲצָה וְהַלֶּחֶם. דְּמֻיּוֹת רְחוֹקוֹת עַל הָאֹפֶק
הַשְּׁלֹשָׁה שֶׁיּוֹשְׁבִים שָׁנִים אֲרֻכּוֹת בְּלִי לִרְאוֹת בְּלִי לִשְׁמֹעַ בְּלִי
לְדַבֵּר שָׁטִים כְּפָטָה מוֹרְגָנָה עַל פְּנֵי הַמִּישׁוֹר שֶׁל חֲלוֹמוֹתַי
וּמַקְפִּיאִים אֶת תְּנוּעַת הַחֶזְיוֹנוֹת מִן הַחוּץ פְּנִימָה. לְלֹא אֱמוּנָה אֲנִי רוֹאָה
דְּבָרִים שֶׁבְּיָמִים אֲחֵרִים הָיוּ מוֹלִידִים אֱמוּנָה וְעַכְשָׁו, כְּאוֹרְחֵי כָּבוֹד מְלַנְכּוֹלִיִּים
לָאֲפֵלָה שֶׁיֵּשׁ בָּהּ מְעַט מַיִם זוֹרְמִים תְּאוּרַת מִסְתּוֹרִין וְעֵשֶׂב נָמוּךְ, אֲנִי חוֹצָה הָלוֹךְ
וָשׁוֹב מְקוֹמוֹת שֶׁנִּתְלוּ מֵעָלַי וְאֵין עֲקֵבוֹת לְמַרְאִית הָעַיִן, לֹא פַּרְסָה לֹא בֹּץ אוֹ כֶּתֶר
נְיָר, רַק לֵב מִתְרוֹקֵן מְהֶפְּנָט מִזְּרִימוֹת הַזְּמַן בִּשְׁעוֹן חוֹל
אֲבָל הַיָּד רוֹעֶדֶת...-
זוֹ שֶׁהוּשְׁטָה לְחַרְצִית אוֹ לְכֶלֶב וְנָגְעָה בְּמִקְרֶה בְּשׁוּלֵי הָרוֹאֶה-הַבִּלְתִּי-נִרְאֶה

Sixth Echo

Every day an angel on the threshold of the room is expecting a call
for a bath and bread. Distant figures on the horizon,
the trio that sits long years without seeing, without hearing, without
speaking, sails like a phantasmagoria on the plain of my dreams
and freezes the passage of visions from the outside to inside. I see without believing
things that in other days might have engendered faith, but now like the darkness's melancholic
guests of honor, in the dark's slow water, mysterious lighting and short grass. I traverse places
that were hung above me. There is no evidence of the visions, no hoof, no mud or paper crown,
only an emptying heart transfixed by the sands of time.
But the hand that reached for the daisy or a dog
touches by chance the hem of the invisible-that-sees,
and it trembles—

ILKA PAPP-ZAKOR was born in Cluj-Napoca, Romania, where she earned a master's degree in Hungarian. Later in Helsinki, Finland, she studied biology and trained rats. Her first book, the short-story collection *Angel Dinner*, was a 2015 JAK-kendő Award winner. She currently lives in Budapest, Hungary.

Anyuka

"Kérlek," mondom, de nem kérek semmit, ez most azt jelenti, hogy legyen meg nektek, sértődött felhanggal, amely egyértelműsíti, hogy neheztelek, mert engem meg sem kérdeztek a dologról. Mondhatjuk azt tulajdonképpen, hogy így nekem is megvan, pár nap múlva pedig csomagolni kezdünk, mert, mint megtudom, a házat tulajdonképpen már el is adták, nagyjából *a fejem fölül*, idézhetném most szegény anyámat. Hallani sem akarnak arról, hogy maradjak, pedig már-már toporzékolok.

"Anyuka," mondja a lányom, "hát így jobban tudunk majd vigyázni rád."

"Anyuka," mondja a férje is, anyukád neked a hétrézfaszú bagoly, gondolom, és hozzávágom a mosogatórongyot. Attól a naptól kezdve nem engednek mosogatni, ebéd után párnákat gyúrnak alám, bekapcsolják a tévét, kezembe adják a távirányítót.

"Anyuka," mondja a lányom férje, akinek nem vagyok anyukája, "volna-e kedve valami kedves kis sorozatfilmhez? Na nézze csak, már be is kapcsoltuk. Hozzak egy cappuccinócskát? Kávécskát nem ihat, anyuka, az rosszat tesz a szívecskéjének."

Ha elfordulok, és úgy teszek, mintha aludnék, akkor se hagyja a rohadt párnát, húzkodja, lökdösi, megpróbálja teljesen a fejem alá tömni, ha ráharapok a kezére, zavartan nevet:

"Anyukád már megint rosszat álmodott, mondja a lányomnak, "főzünk neki finom nyugtató teácskát."

A csomagolást is ők végzik igazából, nekem csak a saját, személyes *holmicskámat* kell összegyűjteni, amihez ők nem értenek, mert számomra . . .

Translated by
TIMEA SIPOS

Mother

"Please," I say, but I'm not asking for anything, I just mean, you win, with an offended tone that makes it clear I'm holding a grudge, because they didn't even ask me about putting the house on the market. I guess we could say that holding a grudge makes me a winner too, but a few days later we start packing up the house because, as I come to find out, they've already sold it, essentially out from under me, to quote my late mother. They don't even wanna hear about me staying, even though I'm practically stomping.

"Mom," my daughter says, "we can take care of you better this way."

"Mom," says her husband. Your mother is the devil himself, I think, and hurl the dishrag at him. From that day on, they don't let me wash dishes anymore. They cram pillows under me after lunch, turn on the TV, put the remote in my hand.

"Mom," says my daughter's husband, whose mom I'm not, "are you in the mood for a nice little TV show? Look here now, I've already turned it on. Should I bring you a little cappuccino? You can't drink coffee, Mom, it's bad for your little heart."

Even if I turn away and pretend like I'm sleeping, he doesn't leave that damn pillow alone. He tugs on it, nudges it, tries to stuff it under my head completely. If I bite his hand, he laughs nervously. "Your mother was having a bad dream again," he says to my daughter. "We'll just make her some nice, hot tea to relax her."

They even finish the packing by themselves. I just have to collect my own, personal little things, which they don't get because they have sentimental value to me, so I'm sitting in the middle of the room on the rug, folding an embroidered handkerchief. I spread it out on my knee with the monogram in the middle. I fold it, and the monogram disappears. I do this several thousand times while my daughter clears out my underwear from my wardrobe and lays them in the suitcase one at a time. If I get up, she says, "Don't you go wearing yourself out now, the trip will be tiring enough as it is."

I thought she meant that I'll get to drive too, but no, she's just afraid that my head will hurt on the long road trip from all the lurching. Well, has my head ever hurt in a car? And on the freeway no less? At least I get to carry my own suitcase outside, true, but only because they're not looking then, so I have to hurry. They twist the next suitcase out of my hand, give me a thermos instead. "This won't be too heavy for you, Mom?" That wasn't my daughter, but her kiss-ass husband.

When we arrive, I think, what a big house, there'll definitely be enough for me to do here. There's a garden, too. I escape behind a tree and yank an aspirin out of my bag, my head aches a little after the several-days-long trip, it would've been better to rest more often. All my life I wanted to garden, surprisingly they agree to it right away. "One to two hours a day, no more than that, Mom," my loving daughter warns me. "Look how hard the sun is shining. Tomorrow we'll go buy you a pretty straw hat."

What does she mean *we'll* buy one? I'll buy it myself. I at least have my own money for the time being, and a mouth too. I'll tell them nicely what I want. I'll bring her a nice hat, too, with a blue ribbon around the rim. We can plant flowers together. It won't be that hard, and we can have some good talks while we work. The sun doesn't shine that strong yet, it's early spring, but you can find straw hats anyway. They're more expensive than I thought, and the clerk is black, I can't exchange a word with him. I use gestures to get across what I'm looking for. He doesn't understand them, takes a different hat off the shelf, felt, but it doesn't matter, this'll be fine, I don't wanna argue. Mortified, I slouch out of the store, I won't be coming back here again either. Of course, I don't buy anything for my daughter in the end, but she doesn't come out to the garden anyway, she

> *I play tug of war with a hornet while I make coffee.*

has to help put the house in order. They clean and unpack together. They organize my room, though every once in a while I steal into the bedroom. Mud falls from my shoes onto the carpet.

"Don't you make a mess now, Mom," my daughter's husband says. "Now look at what a charming little room this is. The ceiling is tilted, like in a house out of a fairy tale. How nice this'll be for you, Mom!"

There's only a chair at my fingertips, and I can't very well hurl that at him. When they leave the room, I rearrange the whole thing. When I'm in the bathroom, they go in and put everything back the way it was.

"Mom, isn't it so much more beautiful this way? It seems so much bigger like this! And so much brighter! We'll even hang a mirror here. It'll be just like a classy salon."

When they leave again, I pull the table over to the other side of the room, I move the standing lamp to the head of my bed, and I draw the black-out curtains closed so it's clear that this is a crypt, not a salon. And even though it's clear, they don't come back anymore. If I go out to help them, they chase me back in.

"Take a rest already, Mom! Aren't you tired?"

Tomorrow they'll be back at work, at least then I'll be able to cook.

I can't cook, the lunch is already there in the fridge. When did my poor daughter find the time for this, too? You just have to heat it up. By the time they get home, I've set the table for them all nice, but it was useless, they've already had lunch in the city.

At least I make my coffee in the mornings. Nobody can make coffee better than me, not even my daughter, she makes it too weak, and let's not even get into her wimp of a husband. Sometimes I make a raid out of cleaning, but they don't notice, my daughter vacuums again at night. If she happened to have had a bad day, she'll look at me accusingly while she does it. I don't dare speak to her then, I go for a walk instead. I'm beginning to get familiar with the neighborhood, for several weeks I've been exploring around here, so it's hard to find a new path.

I play tug of war with a hornet while I make coffee. Every morning it flies into the kitchen, if I chase it away, it comes back. It's as if it knows the layout of our house. If I drive it out the kitchen window, it comes in through the living room, and back through the kitchen from there. I'd regret killing it, but I'm afraid of it, too. Even when I close all the windows, it finds its way in, maybe through the vents. If I'm in the kitchen, I go into my room instead, wait until the buzzing subsides. Sometimes I just rest, because once it hears me rummaging around in the cupboard, it appears out of nowhere, comes at me angrily.

One day my daughter finds a nest developing in one of the bowls. Well, that's why the wasp always comes back no matter how many times we chase it away. Maybe it was already nesting here last year. Or maybe it brooded here, too? Do wasps brood? My daughter says they don't. The nest buzzes angrily under my hand as I break it in chunks off the rim of the plate. The hard, striped insect body slams against the closed windowpane. It tries to break into the kitchen indignantly, as though it can see what I'm doing. The windowpane thumps loudly.

In the evening, my daughter is getting ready to go to the hospital. She'll spend the night there, because they have to run some tests on her, she hasn't been feeling well lately. I would go in with her, but of course she and her husband won't let me, her husband even packs her things for her. I shouldn't make dinner either, or anything, and anyway, I shouldn't get myself worked up. They smile at me like two Cheshire cats. "Don't worry, Mom, don't worry, she just feels a little faint."

I butter some bread for myself and turn on the TV. By the time my daughter's husband gets home, it's long been dark outside. He sits down on the couch too, and we watch a crime drama together. He's not even that dreadful when he doesn't call me Mom. In fact, he's a rather good-hearted, gentle man. That must be why my daughter married him, though I'd prefer it if he had some brains to complement that gentleness of his.

I call her the next day to find out the results of the test, but she doesn't know anything for sure yet either. At night, he comes home late again, frighteningly alone. They're keeping my daughter in the hospital.

"You don't need to worry, Mom, this is Western medicine," he chuckles while he pats my shoulder.

I can't decide if I should worry or not, but I know that my place is by my daughter's side. Even if I can't stay overnight, I should go see her in the morning.

It's impossible for me to get it out of her husband where I need to go. He just keeps telling me not to work myself up, and grinning like he's a hurdy-gurdy player. I call her at the hospital in vain. She doesn't answer, apparently her cell phone died, but I think she just turned it off so that I can't reach her.

In the morning I bundle up a few treats anyway, I try to reach her again, maybe this time I'll have luck. I call her every half hour, but nothing. Later I realize that maybe she's not even in the hospital at all, but then I brush the stupid thought away. When I open the kitchen cabinet, the hornet's angry buzzing welcomes me. It's practically standing in the air at my eye level, behind it, its nest is growing in the bowl again. I admire the blind fearlessness with which it guards its nest, a real mom, I think, closing the cabinet door. I listen to it calm down and fly back to the bowl.

In the afternoon, I call my daughter's husband, apparently there are still no results. At night we sit on the couch again, staring at the crime dramas. You don't need to worry, he says, but it's also possible that he doesn't say it anymore, I already know it by heart.

After a week, my daughter finally comes home, and hugs me encouragingly. "Oh, Mom, I heard you were all worked up over my being gone. What's the point in worrying yourself like that when you know it breaks my heart?"

When I ask her what they've diagnosed her with she waves me off, laughing, oh, nothing serious, I'm gonna rest at home for a while, and then everything will be all right again, why do you have such a restless nature anyway? I can't get more out of her than this: spring fatigue, it'll pass with the first drought. Like when she was a child, I can't carry her burden now either, though in the morning I bring her the breakfast that her husband makes her. I sit down on the edge of the bed and talk to her, but I can see that it wears her out, so I leave. Later, I open her door, but she's sleeping. Even later, when I try the door again, it's closed. At night she sneaks in through the front door like she did as a teenager, hoping I don't notice that she spent the afternoon elsewhere.

The hornet drones in the kitchen. Sometimes I go out to chase it away, but it flies up to the highest shelf where I couldn't even reach it if I stood on a chair. The nest is growing nicely. If I reached over to break it the hornet would buzz at me menacingly.

My daughter hasn't gone to work for several weeks now, and I still don't know what's going on with her. One night I even yelled, not at her but at her husband, but he just sat me down on a chair and brewed me a cup of nice, hot cocoa. The cocoa really did do me good. It's been pouring for several days now, everything is gray, like that damn nest, which is making me more and more nervous anyway. What would happen if the wasp broke into my daughter's room and wreaked havoc there? In times like this, you can't help but see everything in a darker light.

Her husband has been feeding me in the mornings now. I could protest all I want, he'd cut my ham sandwich into pieces anyway. Then I can go into my daughter's room, but only for a half hour so that I don't exhaust her or waste her time if I don't have to. We don't really talk much, though once I asked her what they fight about almost every night. Of course, she didn't answer, she acted like she didn't know what I was talking about and then when she couldn't deny it any longer she just said, yeah, that. I'd rather not work myself up, or her, so I just sit and pet her hand, and she reassures me that everything is okay and soon everything will be back to normal.

While I watch TV in the living room, I hear the familiar buzzing again. The wasp happens to be sitting on the doorframe, cleaning its wings. I close the door and hear a light crunching sound. I really didn't want to kill it, but it was unbearable. It could've stung any one of us at any time. When I inspect the carcass, it seems smaller to me than a hornet, though I can't tell one wasp from another. Just to be safe, I open the kitchen cabinet. It's empty, only the nearly complete nest skulks inside the bowl. Remorse catches up to me. I run from it into my room. I don't harm the nest, there's no reason to now.

At night, they're fighting again. I listen to their yelling and shrieking from my bed. Something cracks, like a chair just fell over. Later, there's a knock on my door, and I prepare for the worst. It's probably my daughter asking with red eyes for permission to come inside and be consoled. But no, it's her husband bringing me a cup of hot cocoa.

Not long after that a new man appears at our place. They don't even introduce me to him, we just pass each other in the hallway. At first I think he's their friend, but then I see him dusting, so he's more like a housekeeper. My daughter's husband says he can't work and take care of the house at the same time. And my daughter, she asked for him, she needs someone capable who can care for the house, she doesn't trust her husband to do it, he neglects everything.

It seems like the newcomer annoys her husband. When he appears in the morning, her husband hurries out the house as if he were fleeing, and the guy starts to clean, cook, and straighten up. He goes into my daughter's room, perhaps to give her medicine, stays until my daughter falls asleep, and I only find the door locked with a key now.

I don't talk to the housekeeper, but I suspect he's probably an arrogant guy, not even a guy, more like a dandy, with his pants that are ironed along the edges, a hardened, white collared shirt and bow tie. Sometimes he even stays at our place overnight, and then he sits with my daughter behind closed doors, and in the hallway only their faint whispering can be heard. So they must know each other from somewhere. I would ask my daughter, but even the slightest hint at the housekeeper bothers her. While the two of them talk, her husband tends to me, makes me cocoa, watches the crime dramas on TV with me.

Before sleep, the thought torments me that maybe I didn't kill the right hornet, but the thought always leaves me by morning. Then one day before lunch, I remember it again. I venture out to the kitchen, where the dandy is washing dishes, and I yank open the cupboard aggressively in front of his nose and spot the beautiful, yellow striped insect as it finishes the final touches on its nest. It belligerently snaps its head up and lunges to attack. I slam the door, and my gaze falls upon the guy. I don't believe what I'm seeing: he's wearing a flower in his buttonhole. A purple-ish carnation, which complicates the situation. White foam and dishwater envelop his gloved hand.

"What a cheap buffoon you are," I tell him, and slap his shoulder in a friendly way. He doesn't know Hungarian, he smiles and nods slightly. From that day on, this is how I turn up my mood. I walk down the hallway, try the handle on my daughter's door, even though I know it's locked, and she wakes up for a second and shouts, hello, Mom, how are you? Wonderful, honey, wonderful, I chirp, then breeze into the kitchen, stop in front of our housekeeper, and announce: "You are a scabby maggot." I endear myself to him, "A pock-marked grave-robber, a deceitful prairie wolf."

I figure he'd understand hyena, so I use prairie wolf. He just stares and smiles, adjusts the flower in his buttonhole that is always a different color, pulls on his hardened shirtsleeves, nods, and says something, perhaps a thank you, perhaps a good morning to you too. Then he proudly continues washing dishes, like someone who knows that everything is perfectly okay.

That night he stays over again. I can hear him sneak into my daughter's room, so I hurry to the bathroom instead. I soak myself in the fragrant bubble bath, and I try not to hear the sobbing beginning to ring out from my daughter's room, the shrieking and yelling, and soon someone tries the handle. It's my daughter's husband, sadly clutching a stool. He doesn't call me Mom anymore, nor does he tell me not to worry, he only sits down next to me, and wets his hand. Something gets knocked over in the room below us, they're screaming without end, and my daughter's husband puts his wet hand on the nape of my neck. For a second I think he's going to push my head under water, but no, he just helps shampoo my hair. Finally, he starts smiling in his tame, modest way. He pulls paper boats out of his pockets, and releases them on the water. "Look, Mom," he says, "I brought these for you. I folded them myself. They're beautiful, right?" He says, and waits for me to praise them. A hornet crawls in through the vent, buzzing, and settles on the edge of the bath to clean its legs.

I like to watch wasps in the summer. They're diligent, proud animals, and one would like to think they have souls too.

NAHID ARJOUNI's poetry is well known for its exploration of femininity and war in the Middle East. She holds a master's degree in psychology and lives in Sanandaj, the Kurdistan region of Iran. She has three poetry books, published in Iran and Arbil, Iraq.

خدای آشپزخانه

ای خدای بزرگ
که توی آشپزخانه هم هستی
وروی جلد قرص های مرا می‌خوانی
!لطفا کمی آن طرف تر
باید همه‌ی این ظرف‌ها را آب بکشم
وهمین طور که دارم با تو حرف می‌زنم
به فکر غذای ظهر هم باشم
!نه کمک نمی‌خواهم
خودم هوای همه چیز را دارم
پذیرایی جارو می‌خواهد
غذا سر نمی رود
به تلفن‌ها هم خودم جواب می‌دهم
...و گردگیری این قاب
یادت هست؟
اینجا کوچک بودم
وتو هنوز خشمگین نبودی
ومن آرامبخش نمی‌خوردم
درست بعد طعم توت فرنگی بود و خواب
که تو اخم کردی
به سیزده سالگی

Translated by
SHOHREH LAICI

Kitchen God

Oh dear God who is always in the kitchen
reading the names of my pill bottles,
please stand back!
I must do the dishes
and cook something for lunch, while
talking with you.
No, no need to help me, No!
I can handle things on my own,
I should vacuum my living room
and I won't serve burnt food,
I will also answer the phone,
and should clean my picture frame, do you remember this photo?
I was a little baby girl in this one
and you were so generous to me,
I didn't take tranquilizers so often!
I could feel your anger after eating strawberries and falling asleep,
the day I was thirteen, those white bed sheets and my dreams...
sorry to be rude,
but you were jealous of my pockets, my girlish purse, and even my
    wooden jewelry box.

ملافه
و رویاهایم
بخش بی پرده می گویم
اما تو به جیب‌هایم
کیف دستی کوچکم
و حتی صندوقچه‌ی قفل دار من
! چشم داشتی
ای خدای بزرگ که توی آشپزخانه‌ام نشسته‌ای
حالا یک زن کاملم
چیزی توی جیب‌هایم پنهان نمی کنم
کیفم روی میز باز مانده است
هر هشت ساعت یک آرامبخش می‌خورم
و به دکترم قول داده‌ام زیاد فکر نکنم
لطفا پایت را بردار
می‌خواهم تی بکشم

Oh dear God who sits in my kitchen!
Now I'm a mature woman and
I don't hide the things in my pockets.
My purse lies open on the table,
and I take one tranquilizer every eight hours
and my doctor has given me a prescription: Do not think
Oh, dear God, please pick up your feet.
I want to scrub the floor!

اُردوگاه

کسي از شنبه ها يمان عکس نمي گيرد
از نگاه هاي شرقي مان در غروب اردوگاه
و زن هايي که مي دانند وطن
!آواز مرده اي ست که برنمي گردد
ما شناسنامه هايمان را برداشته ايم
با ترس هايمان که بزرگ ترند
کسي از ما با چشم هاي بادامي اش گريه مي کند
کسي از ما با چشم هاي درشت
من با چشم هاي جنگ زده ام
پرت مي شوم
به حاشيه ي خبرها
و فکر مي کنم شيميايي شده اند شعرهاي ام
و حنجره اي که با آن بغض مي کنم
مرا به دريا بياندازيد
مي خواهم خوراك کوسه ها بشود صبوري ام
و تصويرهايي از حلبچه
!که خوراك روزنامه هاي وطنم شد
حالا ما
به تمام زبان هاي زنده ي دنيا
... گريه مي کنيم
مرا به دريا بياندازيد
مي خواهم با ماهي سياه کوچکي
که توي کودکي ام بود
!حرف بزنم

Refugee Camp

No one takes photos of our Saturdays,
of our eastern eyes at sunset in the refugee camp.
No one photographs the women who believe
their homeland is a dead, forgotten song.
We have clutched our birth certificates,
and hold our fears so deep.
One of us is crying with her almond eyes,
one of us is crying with big eyes!
I've become the current events, the news,
and I feel like a poet whose poems have been attacked with chemical weapons,
and my larynx, too, with which I cry out.
Throw me to the sea;
I want to feed the sharks with my patience,
like the images of Halabja that fed the media of my motherland!
Now, we cry out in all languages of the world,
Throw me to the sea!
I want to talk with the little black fish of my childhood.

Translated by Shohreh Laici • Persian | Iran

و

مرده

من مرده‌ام
توي يكي از همين زندان‌هاي حاشيه
و نام مردنم را خاموش نوشته‌اند
حالا دلم مي‌خواهد به هياهو برگردم
به لب‌هايت كه نيمه‌ي زندگي من بود
ونيم ديگرم شب‌هاي اين بار شب بخير!
اين بار شب بخي!
شب بخير پرنده‌ي غمگين
كه بوسه‌هاي كوچكت را به ملاقات من آوردي
ودست‌هايت را گذاشتي روي ميله‌ها
تا خورشيد را نديده نميرم

از تيتر مرگ خاموش بدم مي‌آيد
از روزنامه‌هاي دست به عصا هم
واز لبخند رئيس جمهورهاي جنگ

مي‌خواهم به دست‌هاي تو برگردم
به غوغاي شب‌هايي كه كاش صبح نشود
مي‌خواهم براي خودم يك جفت كفش تخت بگيرم
مي‌خواهم شبيه درخت سبز شوم در مسير آمدنت
وحرف‌هاي تلخ را پشت گوش بياندازم
جنگ را
روزنامه را
واين كه خاموش مرده‌ام!

Deaden

I'm dead,
at one of these neighborhood jails
and the name of my death has been inscribed by silence.
My dream wants to recall the sounds,
to remember your lips which were the dream of your life and
the way you whisper Good night, these nights!
Good night, the sad bird
who has given me little kisses.
Place your hands on the prison bars and let me feel the sunlight
before I die.

I hate to die in silence,
I hate to listen to the hard-line media, too,
and the grins of presidents who do nothing but make war!

I want your hands and
the sounds of those endless nights.
I want to become like a tree growing on your path,
heedless of dark thoughts,
such as war,
and my silent death.

Translated by Shohreh Laici • Persian | Iran

من ریشه هایم جایی پیش تو بود

دنیا ی کوچکی ست
تو روز هایت را برمی داری
با تکه هایی از من
که ریخته است روی خاک
من مرزها را
خط می زنم از کتاب ها
!از موهایم که عاشق بود
پدر گفت کوتاهش کن
اصلا ببر صدای این اسب های لعنتی را
ما مال این سرزمین نیستیم می فهمی؟
من تکه ای از زمین را جابجا کردم
کمی از خاک های پدر را آوردم
و ریختم پای شمعدانی ها
و ریختم روی آسفالت های بدقواره ی این شهر
و ریختم توی صورت بچه هایی که
به مادر بزرگ گفتند ارمنی
و می خندیدند
پدر گفت وقتی ریشه هایت جای دیگری باشد
و بعد ادامه نداد
من ریشه هایم جایی پیش تو بود
وشیهه هایم را
تنها اسب های غریبه دوست داشتند
اسب هایی که مال هیچ سرزمینی نبودند
من به ریشه هایم فکر می کردم توی مدرسه
توی مقنعه
وقتی که بوی خون
توی سرود ملی ومارش های پیروزی
دیوانه ام می کرد

My roots were somewhere with you

Such a small world
you spend your days with the broken pieces of me,
fallen to earth.
I delete the borders from the books, from my hair, too;
Father said, "Cut it off."
He added, "Fuck the horses' whinnies, we don't belong to this country! Don't you understand?"
I disturb the earth and spread some of my ancestors' soil near the geraniums,
and throw more on the broken and ugly asphalt of the streets.
I throw it on the face of the child who calls Grandma "foreigner," laughing.
Father said, "It happens a lot when your roots are somewhere else,"
and then he stopped talking.
My roots were somewhere with you,
and only the strange horses loved my whinny, those who belong to no land.
I think of my roots at school, in my headscarf, while the smell of blood in the national anthem
made me deeply sad!
I think it's the earth's stupidity which lets us break it into pieces, borders.
I think it's the politicians' stupidity that never lets soldiers in love fear death in war.
Sometimes I think my teachers are dumb, those who believe war is holy and that not wearing the hijab helps the enemy.
I take out my ponytail in class and the horses shriek.
Father said, "Your roots were somewhere else," and I was thinking of you who are somewhere else.
You hate the blood,
the politicians, too, those who never let soldiers in love fear war.

Translated by Shohreh Laici • Persian | Iran

من فکر میکردم زمین چه قدر ابله است
که می گذارد تکه تکه اش کنند
وسیاستمدارها
که نمی گذارند سربازهای عاشق
شجاع نباشند در مقابل مرگ
من حتی پیش خودم فکر می کردم
حتما توی کله ی خانم مدیر
گچ ریخته اند
که می گوید
جنگ غنیمت است
!و موهای ما به دشمن کمک می کند
من دم اسبی ام را باز می کردم توی کلاس
و اسب ها شیهه می کشیدند
پدر می گفت
وقتی ریشه هایت جای دیگری باشد
من به تو فکرمی کردم که جای دیگری بودی
و از خون بدت می آمد
و از سیاستمدارها
که نمی گذاشتند سربازهای عاشق از جنگ بترسند

GEORGES-OLIVIER CHÂTEAUREYNAUD is a key figure in contemporary France for the fantastic as a genre and the short story as a form. His volume of selected stories *A Life on Paper* (Small Beer, 2010) won the Science Fiction & Fantasy Translation Award and was shortlisted for the Best Translated Book Award.

Une route poudreuse mène d'Argos à Mycènes

Elles tournaient la tête de son côté, avant de revenir à la contemplation obtuse d'un bec de gaz ou d'un banc public. Il ne passait pas d'autos que l'homme à la valise aurait pu arrêter, dont il aurait pu supplier le chauffeur de l'emporter loin de cet effrayant voisinage. Depuis qu'il avait mis le pied hors de la gare il n'avait pas entendu le moindre bruit de moteur. La cité demeurait silencieuse comme un cimetière. On était en fin d'après-midi, et il semblait qu'il n'y eût de vivants, dans toute la ville, que lui et ces deux lionnes qui l'observaient comme à la dérobée.

Il n'osait pas trop les regarder de peur de les provoquer. Il les trouvait belles, d'une beauté suffocante. Le Créateur aurait pu, peut-être même aurait-il dû s'en tenir à elles, s'arrêter là et chiffonner tout le reste. À quoi bon les hippocampes, les caméléons, les hannetons, les zèbres, les chèvres, les requins-marteaux, les chevaux, et même les singes, et même les hommes? La perfection à elles seules, ces deux lionnes auraient suffi, et largement! N'empêche, c'était plus de peur de d'admiration que le cœur de l'homme à la valise battait chaque fois qu'il les apercevait. S'interdisant toute précipitation, il rebroussait chemin ou s'engageait dans une rue adjacente. Sa valise à la main (heureusement elle n'était pas lourde, il y avait fourré le minimum: ses notes pour sa conférence, une rechange de linge de corps, une trousse de toilette...) il se forçait une fois hors de vue à marcher aussi vite et aussi silencieusement que possible. Il s'attendait à chaque seconde à sentir sur sa nuque le souffle chaud d'un fauve, et sur ses épaules le poids écrasant de . . .

Translated by
EDWARD GAUVIN

It's a Long Dusty Road from Argos to Mycenae

They turned their heads his way before resuming their obtuse contemplation of a gaslight or a public bench. Not an automobile passed that the man with the suitcase might have stopped, not a driver he might have begged to take him far away from this terrifying propinquity. Since setting foot outside the station, he hadn't heard the sound of a single engine. The city remained silent as the grave. It was late April, and it seemed not a creature was stirring in all of town save for himself and the two lionesses almost furtively observing him.

He dared not glance their way too often for fear of provoking them. He found them beautiful, staggeringly so. The Creator could have, perhaps should have called it a day, stopped right there and tossed the rest. What was the point of seahorses, chameleons, cockchafers, zebras, goats, hammerhead sharks, horses—even apes, even people? Perfection incarnate, those two lionesses would've sufficed, and then some. Still, whenever the man with the suitcase caught the merest glimpse of them, his heart pounded more from fear than admiration. Refraining from all haste, he turned back and down a side street. Suitcase in hand (luckily it wasn't heavy, he'd packed the minimum: his lecture notes, clean underwear, toiletries), he forced himself, once out of view, to walk as quickly and quietly as possible. He expected at any second to feel, on the nape of his neck, the warm breath of a wild animal, and on his shoulders, the crushing weight of its paws. After a moment, he looked over his shoulder and let out a sigh of relief. The street was empty!

He let himself break into a sprint then, with an eye to putting an entirely desirable distance between himself and the absolute beauty of the lionesses. Alas! He simply ran into them a bit farther on, sprawled placidly across the sidewalk, seemingly indifferent to his presence. You'd think this town was lousy with lionesses, had been his first thought. However, he was soon convinced that it was always the same two. Lionesses aren't interchangeable, like ants. Each has a way about her, a physiognomy entirely her own. It all seemed as if, while he was fleeing them, they'd pursued their course and, deliberate of step, rounded the next block, even the next several, just to pass him and station themselves impassively in his path once more. There was something supernatural about this ubiquity. But eventually, after running into them several times in a row without being attacked, he felt almost reassured. He set out again, in hopes of shaking them sooner or later. And yet at one moment or another, round a bend in the road or upon exiting a square, there they were again, giving him a brief, chilly, sidelong glance.

He'd been shown, before leaving, the way to the Excelsior Hotel where a room had been reserved for him, but with all the detours he'd taken in a vain attempt to escape the lionesses, he'd gotten lost. And not a single passerby turned up along these lifeless streets to give him directions. A dull anger began growing inside him, almost supplanting his fear. What kind of godforsaken hole was this, anyway? Even as he cursed the city, he chastised himself for accepting the far-from-tempting offer—poorly paid—that had led him here. Giving talks on this and that was his livelihood, as a haphazard savant and obscure polymath. But the one he was supposed to give this time, before an audience in bedroom slippers, a codger's club, would add as little to his bank account as to his résumé. He was used to it, though. If offered something in his wheelhouse—in this case a little chat on Mycenaean civilization—if there were a few pennies to be made, if his travel, food, and lodging were paid for, he always said yes without shilly-shallying. Hadn't he a few glimmers to shed on almost any civilization, Mycenaean or otherwise? So here he was: having come in on the 5:30 train, he counted on checking in by 5:45 so he could settle in and unwind before the lecture at 7:00 (seniors slept early). Now it was already 6:30. The city was hardly

He froze, barely breathing, seeking refuge in a statuelike stasis.

large (not even a regional capital), but he had no map in hand, and signage seemed nonexistent.

He decided to call the club director for help. Keeping an eye on the lionesses lolling, at a remove, on the asphalt, he tried to open his suitcase and get his planner. He'd written down the number of the club on today's page. He swore, recalling that he'd locked the suitcase, and wondered why in the world he'd ever done so. Where was that damned key? He rummaged around in his pockets, and his annoyance soon turned to panic: lost, or left at home! Without that number, what good was his cell phone?

If at least he could've ducked into a café, any café...or some store, or even a lobby somewhere! But all the shops were shut up tight, and though it was still early yet, lighted keypads guarded access to all the buildings. He'd tried, he'd even rung up on the intercom. In vain. An idea occurred to him: the police! Two lionesses running free in the heart of the town—now there was a legitimate reason, if ever, for recourse to the forces of law and order. But the second his fingers brushed his phone, a disapproving growl halted him mid-motion. One of the two lionesses was staring fixedly at him, an irate glint in her bright yellow eyes. With fluid grace, she rose to all fours. Good God, the harmonious play of those muscles under the trim coat that outlined her perfect form! As if, in her nonchalance, could be read the certainty of seizing her prey in a single bound... A hiccup of terror escaped him. The other lioness had also gotten to her feet. Both pairs of eyes were now turned on him. He folded his cell phone; the click of the case as it closed gave him a start. Still at a remove—but such a close remove!—the first lioness yawned. Her muzzle wrinkled, then her jaws gaped wide. He saw her fleshy tongue, pink, almost obscene beside the ivory portcullis of her fangs. He froze, barely breathing, seeking refuge in a statuelike stasis. If he could, he would've commanded his whole body to be silent, ordered his heart to stop beating, curtailed all internal activity down to the most infinitesimal organic tremor. The felines did not pounce upon him as he'd feared, and he took courage again. The menacing glint dimmed in those yellow eyes, even as their focus on him grew vague. On the brink of suffocation, he waited till the lionesses lay down again before daring to draw a real breath of air, to let blood flow to limbs and organs once more. With one hand, he sleighted the phone away into a pocket and bent over to grab his suitcase. Was it fatigue, or nerves? The suitcase felt abnormally heavy—heavier, at any rate, than when he'd stepped off the train... Slowly, he skirted the lionesses, moving away with tiny steps. He was almost at the intersection when a new growl, this time furious and hoarse, rose behind him, immediately followed by another and a scraping of claws on asphalt. He let out a feeble, ridiculous little squeak—the squeak of a mouse or a rabbit pursued by a predator, he thought. He clutched the suitcase to himself and took to his heels. He ran without hope, and yet with all his might, as he had never before run in all his life. He ran and ran, incredulity mounting inside him with each passing second. What the hell were they up to? No one could outrun a lioness on open terrain. And yet he seemed to have been running like this for hours. Let it be over with once and for all! Let one of them land on his back, shred his shoulders, shatter his spine, and rip out his jugular!

With the lionesses in hot pursuit, he shot out into a public square. Atop a pedestal on a central island stood a bronze general in a bicorne and epaulettes, one hand brandishing a saber, the other pointing to the façade of the Excelsior Hotel. And miraculously, the hotel's glass doors were wide open! He could not have said from which depths of his soul he dredged up the final scrap of energy that allowed him to reach those doors. It cost him his suitcase. He let it slip from his hands, and it bounced into the paws of his nearest pursuer. The lioness swerved. By doing so she lost the fraction of a second it took her prey to dive into the hotel lobby and shut the door behind him. A resounding boom shook the thick glass pane when the speedier lioness hurled herself at it headfirst. The door opened a crack, but seizing his chance as the half-stunned cat fell back, the escapee slammed the door shut again and turned the latches at the top and bottom. He felt faint then, and collapsed into a sofa near the front desk. Outside, the second lioness collided in turn with the transparent barrier. Her sister returned to press her bloody muzzle and heavy paws to the glass. From her claws came a sinister screech.

The man turned toward the front desk. There was no one behind the counter. The sound of the lions smacking into the door hadn't roused anyone's attention. Was the entire hotel deserted? And yet the door had been open... A gilded bell gleamed on the counter. He rose, dragged himself over, and rang. It let out a tinkle that brought no one running. He rang again, to no greater result. He called out then, in a shaken voice: "Hello? Anyone home? There are lions outside!" Falling silent again, he waited, now and then casting a worried glance over his shoulder. The lionesses were still outside. They paced, growling, before the door. Sometimes one of them would stop and scrutinize the inside of the lobby, a grudgeful glimmer in its eye. Even behind his transparent bulwark, whose sturdiness had been confirmed, he did not feel entirely safe. Not to mention there was hardly any chance he'd give his lecture now, and no oration, no compensation. This trivial thought became part of the anger that flooded him anew. Anger at himself, for getting mixed up in another calamitous mess... At the club that had invited him, at the lionesses, and at the town, at this hotel where no one came when he shouted or rang, at the world, at life, at the heavens!

As his disgusted gaze strayed over the counter, he noticed a room key lying on a sheet of paper. In marker on the sheet, beneath the same number graven on the rubber-ringed copper ball attached to the key, he made out his name. He shrugged aside his wounded pride at seeing his name marred by misspelling, reckoning he could take it for granted that the number, 12, referred to his room, to which the key would logically give him access. Given the number, the room in question was likely on the second floor. He decided to go up and see. Before stepping away, the receptionist had no doubt left the key in an obvious place so he would find it. Upstairs, he could refresh himself after the chase that had drenched him in sweat. He gazed past the heads of the lionesses still prowling in circles outside the door, and gave his suitcase one last apologetic, sorrowing glance. There it was, sitting in the middle of the street. He was afraid a car would run it over, if any came by. Not that there was anything valuable inside; it wasn't even new. But it undoubtedly had a few years left in it.

He pictured the retirees at the club, astonished by his lateness, at first wondering and then indignant.

He grabbed the key and went upstairs. It was a modest hotel. He wasn't one of those celebrated scholars whom cultural powers put up in palaces. Two stars, sometimes even one, was good enough for him.

The room was just as he expected: small, clean enough, bright enough, livable enough. With a sigh of satisfaction, he locked himself in, the door yet another obstacle between him and the lionesses. He took off his shoes and jacket, sat down on the bed to rub his feet, rose, went into the bathroom, washed his hands, and splashed water on his face. Then he went back to the bed, pulled the covers aside, plumped the pillows, lay down on his back, and shut his eyes. He would've liked to dive headlong into sleep. He'd have sunk straightaway, as a lead-limbed shipwreck victim gives up hope of staying long afloat in this grueling world. But the thought of his suitcase at the mercy of car wheels or some dishonest pedestrian kept him awake. And then there was the missed lecture. They would be waiting for him. He pictured the retirees at the club, astonished by his lateness, at first wondering and then indignant. Disappointed, cheated out of a promised intellectual jaunt beneath an Attic sun, they'd go sadly back to their TVs and their dominos, never climbing the acropolis in Mycenae under his care, never stepping through the Lion Gate... The sound of an engine finally tore him from his drowsiness. He leaped to his feet and rushed to the window. A small, gaily-colored van—the first vehicle he'd seen since he arrived—slowed as it reached the square. Smack in the middle by the statue, one of the lionesses—the ringleader—was rolling with disarming abandon atop his suitcase. Though he was far away and his window shut, he thought to hear her purring with pleasure. The other lioness, as if jealous, stalked around her. The van came to a stop. A bareheaded woman got out, her one-of-a-kind dolman open on a tiny tank top and jeans. She opened the back door, grabbed a long whip, gave it a crack, and marched resolutely toward the big cats. The situation was now clear: the lionesses had escaped from the circus and their owner had set out looking for them in street clothes, taking just enough time to throw on her tamer's outfit... Far from obeying her commands and climbing meekly into the van, the lionesses responded with growls at first, baring their teeth. Then, as the lion tamer continued her advance, they regretfully relinquished the suitcase they seemed to love so much and took off, as if they'd planned it in advance, in diametrically opposed directions. Already they had disappeared, the ringleader around a corner, the other leaping over the gate to a small courtyard where shrubbery hid her instantly from sight.

With impotent rage, the lion tamer cracked her whip once more before tossing it in the back of the van and closing the doors. She retraced her steps, bent over, and with a baffled look hoisted the suitcase. In the room above, the man opened the window and shouted, "Ma'am! Hey! Over here! Ma'am! That's mine! That's my suitcase! I'll be right down!" The woman looked his way and made as if to hoist it aloft, but stopped halfway as if it had proven too heavy.

The man tossed on his jacket in a hurry. Not even bothering to tie his shoes, he dashed out of the room and tore downstairs at the risk of tripping over his own laces. A few seconds later, he'd reached the lion tamer at the base of the statue. She held out his suitcase. He grabbed it. For a brief moment, he doubted it was his, it seemed so heavy. But a cracked and wrinkled sticker, bas-relief from an already ancient flight, attested to the fact that it was his. The lion tamer scowled and checked her watch. The way things were looking, she had no chance of getting her animals back in time for the show. For his part, the man could kiss his lecture and his honorarium goodbye unless... He explained that they were expecting him at the seniors' club on... The name of the street eluded him. By chance, the lion tamer had driven right by it, a handsome historic townhouse, while looking for her lions. He was astonished. Usually seniors' clubs were in shabby prefab buildings. "So they're waiting for you?" asked the lion tamer. "Climb in, I'll give you a ride!"

She dropped him off in front of a stone building fit for a government ministry, or even the main branch of a Swiss bank. An inscription engraved on the façade indicated the purpose of the edifice. "Don't forget your suitcase!" the lion tamer said as he was getting out of the van. Rather than lose the few minutes it would've taken to haul it up to the room, he'd brought it with him. It seemed heavier and heavier each time he lifted it, but for now he had other things to worry about. The lion tamer left him beneath a fringed canopy, supported by gilded poles, that sheltered a scarlet carpet leading to the club entrance.

As he stepped into the lobby, a little man on the verge of a nervous breakdown hurried toward him. "There you are at last! We'd given up hope!" The lecturer stammered a few excuses; the little man nodded without listening. "Well, you're here! That's the important thing. Your audience is waiting. No time to stop by your dressing room. We'll leave your bag at the coat check."

He thought he was dreaming. Dressing room? If he'd been on time, he'd have gotten a dressing room? The coat check was in a kind of apse heavy with lacquered wood and brass rods, supervised by a mahogany desk where a young woman sat in a black suit and white shirt. In exchange for his suitcase, she handed him a yellow ticket. When she tried to stow it, the expression on her face betrayed her surprise at its unexpected weight. But the lecturer was already being ushered away. A murmur of relief gradually rippled through the audience at his entrance into the sold-out theater. About three hundred people, he estimated—seniors, to be sure, but not only were there more of them, they were of an entirely different social class than he was used to. Here it was all three-piece suits and ties, pocket squares, lapel pins from various honorary legions, or else custom-made designer dresses, necklaces, cameos, and perms. He felt intimidated, and missed the nice little retirees who usually made up his audiences, men in knit cardigans and sweatpants baggy at the knees, women in flowered dresses and support stockings. He'd always believed that for every man comes a crucial moment of accomplishment or annihilation, and he knew his hour had sounded. Here it was, before this stiff and formal audience of whetted appetite, unimpressed by his usual tricks as a professional prattler, that he would confront the ordeal written into his destiny. Well at ease in their seats of gilded wood and garnet plush, these people would be his judges. According to the verdict they handed down, he would know what his time on this earth had amounted to: a laudable performance or pathetic slapstick. Careful not to step on his trailing laces, he climbed onstage after the man who'd greeted him. There was a smattering of polite applause. He waved. His heart was pounding. The hundred, no, the thousand talks he'd given in the past had served only to prepare him for this one. Approaching the podium they'd set out for him, he thought at first that fright would keep him from uttering so much as a word. He opened his mouth, and realized: not at all. He greeted the audience naturally, effortlessly. His voice rang out loud and clear in the silence that had fallen once more. The microphone had been properly adjusted with respect to volume as well as height and angle, but he could just as easily have done without it. He'd been unable to arm himself with his notes, inaccessible in his suitcase, but he was unruffled, certain of his mastery over his subject. He pressed his hands to the podium, on either side of the sacramental glass of water and carafe, and paused for a beat to gather himself behind closed eyes, before beginning, "Ladies and gentlemen, it's a long dusty road from Argos to Mycenae..."

When, two hours later, he fell silent, the audience, utterly transported, gave him a standing ovation. He bowed, one hand over his heart. The sweat of glory pearled at his temples. All his life, he had been waiting for this moment. He straightened and looked up at the ceiling, where sculpted allegories seemed to be leaning in to congratulate him. He closed his eyes, intoxicated by the cheers that kept flooding in, an unsubsiding swell. At last, with a delighted buzzing, the crowd withdrew. He remained unmoving, eyes closed, wobbly with happiness behind his podium. After a while, no longer hearing a sound, he opened his eyes again. Everyone was gone. He was completely alone. The lights began to dim. He stepped down from the stage and headed for the exit as the final spotlights went out. The lobby was deserted. His suitcase was sitting on the mahogany desk of the coat check, whose shelves and hangers were empty. He was surprised to be abandoned so quickly after his lecture had met with such success. But after all, what did it matter? This triumph made up for all the failures and half-failures, all the disappointments of the past. He bore it within, running through his veins like fresh blood, a pledge of vigor and joy no matter what life now held in store.

He tossed the yellow ticket on the desk and took back his suitcase. He noticed, without much surprise, that he had a very hard time lifting and carrying it. This was somehow, obscurely, in order. He now had to grip it with both hands, and it was a safe bet the handle wouldn't last long. To keep it from breaking, he undertook to carry the suitcase from below, hugging it in his arms. Even like this, the effort was almost beyond him. A decent-sized anvil couldn't have weighed more. He tottered across the lobby, taking tiny steps, and pushed through the revolving door. When he emerged beneath the canopy, every window in the building was dark. The seniors' club and even the street itself were sunken in gloom. The night was surprisingly black. It occurred to him that none of the nights he'd known till now had really deserved the name, but this time, yes, it was truly night, a night so deep and thick it was almost palpable. And in this night, right beside him, with a glow that was a reflection of no other, shone only the eyes of the lionesses. He tightened his grip on his burden, and struck out, best guess, in a direction he supposed was toward his hotel. Shoelaces still dragging behind him, he set his course by the fugitive glimmers of light thrown off by the eyes of the lionesses who preceded him and turned around, from time to time, to be sure he followed.

Palaiseau, June 2011

One of the foremost poets and performance artists of her generation, **ROCÍO CERÓN** combines poetry with sound experimentation, performance, and video. Her volumes of poetry include *Basalto* (2002), *Imperio/Empire* (2008), *Tiento* (2010), *Diorama* (2012), and *Borealis* (2016). Her poems have been translated into many European languages.

América

Se llamaban Krusevac, ahora Cruz. Los edificios transpiraban. Era una isla o un monte cubierto por chozas. Cosa de hombres. Las mujeres guardaban papas, construían el mundo. Cosa de tiento insulso, se pensaba. Paisajes de tonada suave con acordeón de fondo. Astucia. Proa que acumula sal. *Toma mi brazo, corta el ligamento: necesito dejar el gusto por el ajvar.* Callaron las aves a su paso. Remo. En el fondo, los peces intuían. Algunos fosos guardan familias enteras. Pero ellas son salvas. Todas las lenguas de Europa desaparecieron. Tierra. El dulce de manzana no trae olor a clavo. Cada letra deletrea una estancia. Estas mujeres son mis madres. Desde ese día—América—la piel de mis mejillas es llanura.

Translated by
ANNA ROSENWONG

America

Their name was Krusevac, now it's Cruz. The buildings sweat. It was an island or a mountain covered in shacks. Men's affairs. Women tended potatoes, built the world. Care a dull affair, the thinking went. Melancholic landscape melodies with accordion in the background. Cunning. Boat's prow gathering salt. *Take my arm, cut the cord: I must give up my taste for ajvar*. The birds fell silent as they passed. Oar. Deep down, the fish could tell. Some ditches hold entire families. But these women are spared. All the tongues of Europe disappeared. Land. The apple jam carries no whiff of clove. Every letter spells a sojourn. These women are my mothers. Since that day—America—the skin of my cheeks the plains.

Todo exacto, piedra sobre piedra, bajo el estupor. Tengo adherida a la piel—planta del pie—un nombre preciso, una esquirla dentada (aguijón o filo o tenso nudo), cristal a la uretra. Guardo una voz que es sombra, carta y anunciación: América se hunde. Hay una montaña o casa frente al mar que esconde un secreto. *Manto, el desierto es manto.* Se escucha una bestia colmada de fraguas: negros y blancos inventando heredad. Tengo en las manos un país del que he sido arrojada. Cinco millones de emigrantes caben en la cuenca de una sangre común. América es una madre que mata.

Everything just so, brick by brick, beneath the stupor. Stuck to my skin—the sole of my foot—a precise name, a jagged shard (thorn or blade or taut knot), glass to the urethra. I harbor a voice that is shadow, missive, and annunciation: America goes under. There's a mountain or house facing the sea and guarding a secret. *Cloak, the desert is a cloak*. The sound of a beast bursting with forges: black and white inventing inheritance. In my hands I hold a land from which I've been expelled. Five million emigrants fit in the basin of a common blood. America is a murderous mother.

Herrumbre. Contener el puño. La gravedad de las últimas hojas y la nieve. Escucha el resoplido insular. Tan lejos y cercano. El mar brilla para todos pero cerca del carbón sólo resta el miedo. Defendernos de. Acentos sonoros recuerdan a Siberia. Crudo, el frío. Pero en Siberia nunca llega el otoño. Aquí—casi temblando—hay que ir codo con codo. Aquel jardín o muro o tierra nueva. Hacer la América. Herrumbre: desde Portobelo y hasta la Patagonia. Acero sin distinciones. *A ojo se hace el tiento.* El polvo ensombrece las extensiones de tierra. Lentitud entre los pasajeros: pegar el oído al subte, algo se inflama. Algo ya marca el cuerpo.

Rust. Restraining the fist. The gravity of the last leaves and the snow. Hear the insular wheezing. So far and near. The ocean shines for everyone but at close quarters with coal only fear remains. Defending ourselves from. Sonorous accents recall Siberia. Raw, the cold. But in Siberia autumn never comes. Here—almost shivering—we must go arm in arm. That garden or wall or new land. Making America. Rust: from Portobelo all the way to Patagonia. Undifferentiated steel. *Venturing forth by sight.* Dust clouds stretches of earth. Slowness amid the passengers: pressing an ear to the subway, something swells. Something already marking the body.

América es un desierto sonoro. Cazuela de ave levanta muertos, ají de gallina abre sosiego o trucha arcoíris empina rubias. Oscuras nubes modulan temperamentos de valle y bufeo. Crujido de lastras de Machu Picchu—oscuro oficio éste de ser santa. *Yo tenía una tierra, me despojaron de ella, ahora hay un parque de diversiones: juegos replican la muerte y son la muerte.* Algo en la vereda (zanjita, zanja devuélveme el tino, la cara cierta de mi tierra) es sepultura y nacencia. Aguachile que bulle en la quijada. Cacao herido que trae consigo tintineos de piedra. Cárcamo de agua de Tláloc, chacras marítimas de Manantiales. *Cabo Polonio en mi memoria.* Y la fuente que no deja de abastecer el mate seco, verdoso, que enjuaga la voz de la abuela.

America is a sonorous desert. Bird stew to raise the dead, ají de gallina the key to calm, or rainbow trout with lots of beer. Dark clouds regulate the disposition of valley and river dolphin. The creaking slabs of Machu Picchu—a dark business this is, being a saint. *I had a land, they stripped me of her, now there's an amusement park: games play at death and are death.* Something on the trail (ditch, tiny ditch, give me back my good judgment, the true face of my land) is burial and birth. The sizzling of aguachile against the jaw. Wounded cacao that carries with it tinkling stone. Tláloc's gushing fount, Manantiales' oceanside farms. *Cabo Polonio on my mind.* And the fountain that never stops replenishing the dry, green mate washing over my grandmother's voice.

Dijeron que era hija del golpe, de los barrios donde los sones son lentos y carraspean las voces y los toneles de aguardiente se empujan sin trozo de pan; dijeron que era hija del desprecio, de esclavas, de amargas noches de cama entre soldados y cuerpos cobrizos; dijeron que era una mártir—*estaban, están equivocados*—luego le dieron algo de espejos y algo de carne de cerdo, algo de nuevos nombres y nuevos apellidos; le enseñaron el uso de la rueda (ya conocía el cero); casi la mata la fiebre. Y de cada golpe ha salido más fuerte. Como el poema, América es *una dura cicatriz en el cuerpo.*

They said she was born of blows, of barrios where sounds move slow and voices rasp and barrels of aguardiente are tossed back without a bite of bread; they said she was the daughter of disdain, of slaves, of bitter nights in the beds of soldiers and copper-colored bodies; they said she was a martyr—*they were, they are wrong*—and then they gave her some mirrors and a bit of pork, some new first names and new last names; she taught them to use the wheel (she already knew about zero); she almost died of fever. And each blow has made her stronger. Like a poem, America is *a hard scar on the body.*

La Hispaniola. Como si fuera la primera tierra. Que es. Y en ese recuerdo cupieran ya todas las noches de América. Rastro. El ron mantiene a los hombres embrutecidos, me digo. *Mi abuela reza con el vaso de vodka junto, orar es mentirse a uno mismo, me dice, pero conforta el alma.* Como el destilado de oro falso. Nacimiento. Como cadalso al que se entrega uno con la boca abierta, deseosa de alimento naufrago. Montar la oveja, me digo. Ahora los tenis Ducati, el floro que trae de gracia una hembra *ke buena*, las cadenas de oro al cuello, la camisa fina, la marca atrapando al cuerpo, gritando proveniencia. América se hunde, y nadie se ha dado cuenta. La ~~otra América~~ le ha chupado el seso.

Hispaniola. As if it were the first land. Which it is. And as if inside that memory fit all the nights of America. Rum keeps men numb, I tell myself. *My grandmother praying with a glass of vodka in hand, to talk to god is to lie to yourself, she told me, but it comforts the soul.* Like distilled fool's gold. Birth. Like gallows to which you surrender—mouth open, gasping for castaway nourishment. Mounting sheep, I tell myself. Now Ducati sneakers, the smooth talk that gets a chick into bed *ke buena*, gold chains around the neck, fancy shirt, name brand ensnaring the body, screaming provenance. America goes under, and no one's noticed. The ~~other America~~ has sucked its brains.

Dame un tostado. Una jerga que mantenga las cuerdas vocales de mi lengua. Quiero un trapecio. Flotar en él. Quiero la astucia que da la cafeína. Sumergirse en. La otra tierra. Galones enteros. Miles de litros de sangre. Quiénes eran y quiénes son. Todos situados sobre una cuerda. Precipicio. Desde las ruinas de la lengua una tesitura arrogante. Hay una franja de tierra sin nombre. En el fondo de la taza, me dice una gitana en el Parque Forestal, hay una imagen: hombre que aún recuerda a su hija. *Detente, la otra tierra y ese perfil masculino que apenas resulta de las sombras.* Serbia era cobijo—Atlántico—hoy es un lago. Idea del lago.

Give me a dark roast. A vernacular that holds the vocal cords of my language. I want a trapeze. To float on it. I want the edge that caffeine brings. To sink into. The other land. Whole gallons. Thousands of liters of blood. Who they were and who they are. All of them arrayed on a wire. Precipice. Out of the ruins of a language an arrogant tessitura. There's a strip of land with no name. At the bottom of your cup, a gypsy in the Parque Forestal tells me, is a picture: a man who still remembers his daughter. *Halt, the other land and that masculine profile scarcely visible amid the shadows.* Serbia was a refuge—Atlantic—today it's a lake. Idea of the lake.

De la tumba una flor. Plástico decolorado, tierra. Grobnica–París. De Europa sembradío nucas cisternas donde guardar vestigios. Neblina y carbón. Heno y draga, flotantes. Antes del roce sargazos, reflujo luminoso de rostros. Toda la familia astillada. Óleo de museo. Cementerio y nicho para ahondar en el nervio. Cauce púrpura, plantación de cuerpos en otros cuerpos. Cauterio. Atravesar el bosque: mucha fe en los labios. *Ni el uniforme salva.* Allá, en el Golfo de México, secretan zumbantes las aves. Caverna o cardo. Mar gasa, llave al pliegue. La superficie del agua recuerda a los muertos. —Desvanecerse, entre las arrugas de cada pliegue de la madre. *Contenga el aire. Pulmón. Respire profundo. ¿Siente dolor? ¿Siente aquí, sí justo aquí? Es el miedo atrapado. Es América atada en cada corva.* Astilla, flor recogida en Kalemegdan. Y en cada esquina la imagen de un jardín hecho de voces.

From a grave a flower. Faded plastic, dirt. Grobnik–Paris. From Europe sown field napes cisterns safeguarding remains. Mist and coal smoke. Hay and dredge floating. Before the carèss, sargassos, the luminous ebbing of faces. The whole family splintered. Museum oil painting. Graveyard and niche to dig deep into nerve. Purple waterway, plantation of bodies in other bodies. Cautery. Making your way through the forest: devout faith on your lips. *Not even the uniform will save you.* There, in the Gulf of Mexico, the buzzing birds secrete. Cavern or thistle. Gauze sea, key at the fold. The water's surface remembers the dead. —To dissipate amid the wrinkles of every one of the mother's folds. *Hold your breath. Lung. Breathe deep. Do you feel pain? Feel it here? Right here? That's trapped fear. That's America bound at every joint.* Splinter, flower picked in Kalemegdan Park. And at every corner the image of a garden made up of voices.

Los platos vacíos. En el fondo, el campo de gravedad es el tono. El azul. No azul sino provincia y rastro, donde hemos dejado—*Eleonora* flotante a la mirada. Cielo. La mirada hace la patria. *Su país se le ensancha se le gesta se le encima.* América no es orquídea ni animal o pariente. *Tersa era la voz de la abuela.* América deambula entre franjas. Acarrea agua sucia. Retoña entre la mierda. América madre. América padre. *Ofrenda algo. Ofrenda algo de cuerpo a la Pachamama. Entra a esta tierra y hazte un orificio en la lengua.* Forma y pasaje en el sermón de las piedras. Nudo ciego entre ríos. Cordillera. Tu piel—Atacama & Sonora, es concentración, vueltas en círculo, cartografía y nudos. Siglo.

Empty plates. In the background, the gravitational field is the tone. The blue. Not blue but province and trace, where we've left—*Eleonora* floating before the gaze. Sky. The gaze creates the homeland. *Your country swells, arises, overtakes.* America is no orchid, no animal nor kin. *Flowing was the grandmother's voice.* America wanders between borders. Carries dirty water. Blossoms out of shit. Mother America. Father America. *Sacrifice something. Sacrifice something of your body to Pachamama. Enter into this earth and make a hole in your tongue.* Form and passage in the Sermon on the Mount. Blind knot between rivers. Cordillera. Your skin—Atacama & Sonora, is concentration, spinning in circles, cartography and knots. Century.

PATRICK GOUJON grew up in the outskirts of Paris. By turns scenarist, workshop instructor, and short film editor, he is also a frequent participant in writers' residencies. He has worked as a school counselor, and regularly collaborates with young audiences. *À l'arrache* is his fourth novel.

À l'arrache

Ils ont plus peur que vous, j'ai dit aux gamins.

C'est pas tant ça, s'est empressée de me corriger la monitrice, *c'est plutôt que ce sont des animaux qui sentent la peur de l'autre, et ils peuvent en profiter. Ils ont besoin que vous leur montriez qui commande.* Hermann a bombé le torse aussitôt. *Après, c'est vrai aussi que les chevaux sont peureux, et que leurs seuls moyens de défense, c'est soit ruer avec les sabot, soit prendre la fuite.*

Alban piétinait dans la poussière, en triturant, anxieux, le lisère de son tee-shirt. Son regard agité sautait d'un box à l'autre. Il affichait un sourire pincé et répétait, pour se donner une contenance, *Trop des flipettes les chevaux! Ah ouais...* en jouant des épaules. *Moi je préfère carrément les lions.*

Quand il a fallu choisir la monture, les plus téméraires lui ont soufflé les premières places. Un poney pour Fatou et Caddie, et le privilège aux grands de se décider parmi trois chevaux. Adama a opté pour Allégresse, parce que ça sonnait bien; Hermann pour Flambeur parce que c'était le cheval le plus bling-bling ; Alban, du coup, se trouvait d'office obligé d'adopter Débandade. Quoi lui répondre quand il a ronchonné *Débandade? C'est une blague? C'est pourri ce nom, j'en veux pas!*

Hermann et Adama se sont bidonnés, surtout quand Adama, passant la tête dans le box de Débandade, a interpellé Hermann *Choume!* et tous les deux, d'abord choqués par l'érection du cheval, en ont rajouté une couche *T'inquiète, il porte pas bien son nom!*

Faut grandir, les gars, les a mouchés Fred.

Vas-y, il va me porter le mauvais œil! Je le laisse au garage, moi. . . .

Translated by
NOAH M. MINTZ

À l'arrache

They're more afraid than you are, I told the kids.

It's not so much that, the instructor hurried to correct me, *but rather that these animals can smell fear, and take advantage of it. They need you to show them who's in charge.* Hermann immediately stuck out his chest. *Still, it's also true that horses are easily scared, and their sole means of defense is either to kick with their hooves or run off.*

Alban shuffled his feet in the dust, anxiously kneading the hem of his shirt. His restless gaze jumped from one stall to the other. He wore a stiff smile and repeated, to put up a front, *Horses are for pussies! Yeah...* shrugging his shoulders. *I like lions way more.*

When it came time to choose a mount, the more adventurous ones blew past him. A pony for Fatou and Caddie, and for the older boys, the privilege of choosing between three horses. Adama opted for Elation, because that sounded good, Hermann for High Roller because that was the most "bling-bling," so Alban found himself obligated to take Softy. What was there to say when he grumbled *Softy? That a joke? That name sucks, I don't want it.*

Hermann and Adama laughed their heads off, especially when Adama, sticking his head in Softy's stall, called out *Fugly!* to Hermann, both laying it on thick at the sight of the horse's erection: *Don't worry, he don't live up to his name!*

Grow up, boys, Fred put them out.

C'mon, he gon' give me bad luck. I'ma leave him in the garage.

But the instructor lifted the latch and entered Softy's stall to pet his mane. *You're going to hurt his feelings. He's sweet, really, very obedient. Watch. When he's got his ears back it means he's not happy, now he's all right.*

He seems especially happy on the left.

Come on, don't worry, big guy, she added. *First, I'll show you where the equipment is, and then we can begin taking care of them.* She turned toward Fred and me. *Will you be riding, too, or would you prefer to accompany them on foot?*

I'm good, I shot back. *It'd be great to ride, but I'll be more useful on the ground, so I can take pictures.*

I was staring at Softy's inexpressive eyes, and slowly I felt the old fear welling back up, prying into my chest.

WITH THE WISDOM OF our ten years, we assessed the horses warily.

There's no point being scared. They see you bigger than you are. Rodolphe—instructor extraordinaire, the guy who'd been there and done that—had explained to us, tickling the pony between the ears and nostrils. *For him, you're giants. They're more afraid than you!*

I had heard a theory along those lines before, but about elephants, a comic strip I'd seen was coming back to me where a colossal pachyderm gets the crap scared out of it by a mouse. Still, I wasn't going to try and clarify the matter: Rodolphe couldn't stand being contradicted. With a show of nonchalance, he pet the animal's cheek. *Just think, you little fellow, you're upsetting the children! They don't realize you're the one who's freaking out right now!*

Sandra, Benjamin, Flore, and myself were hanging back at least six feet. We were tearing up blades of grass, and I would have preferred to spend all day clearing the entire property than approach the nags that were supposedly afraid of us. True to form, Flex was the only exception. Of course he encouraged me, he who tamed the project's mangy dogs; Flex kicked the asses of those unvaccinated Rottweilers that bared their teeth, revealing a mouth full of fangs. *Ponies are stupid,* he said to Rodolphe, *can't we ride a real horse?*

Let's see what you can do with this one first, hotshot!

The arrival of the equestrian center's instructor calmed us all down, me especially. By way of an introduction, she had declared, *It's normal for you to be intimidated. These are very impressive animals!*

I bridled Diana, inserted the bit into her slimy mouth, passed the headpiece behind her ears, then under her throat. She champed at the bit, and it clinked between her teeth, the steel dripping with drool. Her hooves tore at the wet grass, and each time she shook her rump I worried that she would start kicking.

Rodolphe had slipped a piece of straw between his lips and was acting like a macho cowboy, though in reality he was just an affected pip-squeak with a little blond powder puff on his head; he kept an eye on his herd, paying particular attention to me, his sarcasm blatant when he mocked me: *Come on!* drawing it out like *Come oooooon... The little animal isn't going to eat the big one!*

First of all, I wanted to point out, *that's something you say about spiders or wasps, you moron, not for animals that actually are bigger than you.* But instead I ran my hands over the damaged leather saddle, observing how the others went about harnessing it. Flex had already placed his foot in the stirrup, and with a leap and a thrust, he found himself on the back of his steed.

Sandra, Benjamin, and the others followed his lead. Not me. Paralyzed. *Come ooooon, you gotta get over your fear sooner or later!*

My pulse was thumping behind my eyelids. Uncontrollable. I begged Flex for any words of assurance, but he blew me off, too busy spurring Avalanche's flanks. The instructor was adjusting the straps on the breast of Sandra's horse and Rodolphe was already approaching me, savoring in advance how he would explain to me, seriously and rigorously, what a man is, a real man, before informing me of the barriers that would decidedly keep me from becoming one.

●●●

OOH DAMN, ALBAN'S SHAKING!

Bullshit, I am!

You gonna piss yourself or what? Even Fatou could show you a thing or two!

I'm telling you, just shut up! I'm not scared!

You a thoroughbred, or what?

Alban kept repositioning himself in his saddle, and to top it off, when Softy swatted at the flies on his hindquarters with his tail, he very nearly fell flat on his face. *Whoa, what are you doing?* Alban shouted, giving a shove to the horse's breast, making him all the more agitated. I took my place beside him, without letting the others notice. Fred was steering Fatou's apparently recalcitrant pony, impossible to get out of its stall. Two girls dressed like equestrian riders—they couldn't have been older than twelve—came to lend a hand, and in ten seconds the whole matter was sorted out. The instructor introduced them as her assistants, who would be accompanying us during the ride. Despite their age they were trustworthy and knowledgeable; on the undulating plastic roofing the sun subtly cast its rays, projecting shadows of the pigeon droppings along with the celestial dust, dappling the velvet of the girls' black riding helmets and falling on the studded wooden boards, on the barley, the oats, the bran in the troughs, the soft hay with dark yellow spots.

> *Rodolphe lifted me back up abruptly.* C'mon, get back on! What do we do when we fall off the horse? *he declared.*

The mini-equestrians guided the ponies across the ring and outside the stable. Alban gripped the reins tightly, like the handlebars of a moped. Softy complied with a calm and steady gait. Without looking at Alban, I could feel his stress running through my body. He saved face by staying silent, but there was no need for a sixth sense to feel the fear that emanated from him like an aura.

It'll be okay, I told him for the umpteenth time, and as I walked at Softy's pace I breathed deeply in and out—that old remedy—channeling and purging the inexpressible tension, shame, and pain.

●●●

FALLING FROM DIANA, landing right on my coccyx, I got the wind knocked out of me.

I was crying, shit I was crying, and examining the scratches on my stinging hands without even seeing them.

I pulled my leg out from the stirrup, where it had remained trapped, and mentally cursed this goddamn horse, then applied the same penalty to the sweet instructor who had extolled the generosity of her fucking hoofed meat, as well as my mother for having the bright idea to enroll me in camp, plus this unfair body nature had given me, incapable of maintaining its balance or taking a pummeling, and, last of all, holding back tears, I would have beaten this body up if it weren't mine, or if it at least would have been able to handle that. And also Rodolphe, whose grown-up advice was drowned out by my gasping.

Not a damn thing to do, just deaf and dumb pain.

*Deep breaths in and out...*repeated the center instructor, except that, hey, not even this pain, not a damn thing, my jammed spine is nothing, the impact wasn't the worst of it, the impact, for all the bawling in public I would have tripled its intensity, if only that would buy off some of the weakness, ended some of the bullying, some of Bastien and Farid, the twelve days of camp—*What a little homo!*—the kicks to the ass, the stolen cap, the Coke poured in my toiletry case, to the point where Flex beats them up, if only it would fix Anaïs dancing with all the boys except me, resorting to all kinds of ploys not to have to speak to me in public, if only you could trade pain for pain.

Rodolphe lifted me back up abruptly. *C'mon, get back on! What do we do when we fall off the horse?* he declared. But no. I was stuck in my fear. And it was then, the first in a long series of him calling me *ma pauvre chérie*, my poor darling.

Ma pauvre chérie, *if you do that for everything in life, you'll never stop!*

I don't wanna! I said.

Oh, I don't wanna! he shot back. *Well then,* ma pauvre chérie, *no one's gonna make you.*

●●●

ALBAN AND I WERE moving along at the back. He had calmed down, and Softy, apart from the few inopportune stops he allowed himself to graze at the wild grass on the edge of the trail, was exemplary.

There we go, you guys are buddies! I said to Alban.

Yeah, yeah, he grumbled. *But this horse is too hungry.*

He pulled on the reins with sharp jerks and spurred the animal's flanks, and it worked, and the pride he took from it, judging by the princely bearing he adopted, was immense, I caught it on the camera, immortalized the success etched on a cocky face in a halo of backlighting.

Show me! he demanded, leaning carefully over the camera screen. *Delete*, he could say, or *That one's dope, keep it!* And digitally it was trash or treasure. *See, y'get used to it eventually.*

No, but I wasn't scared, he corrected me.

I know.

It's just, you know, when you ain't done something before...

You gotta get used to it...

Exactly.

Exactly.

Softy started up a tentative trot, stopped short in his tracks.

The others front like they ain't scared, but it's the same thing. It's normal for you to be scared, you're old... I mean, you're grown up, you're an adult. But them, they so full of themselves. I'ma laugh when they got to gallop, or jump over obstacles.

I don't think they're going to have us do hurdles.

Aw, that's too bad, they woulda smashed they faces in.

And me, I would've been the last to want to do it.

You don't like it?

I'm terrified of horses.

The little blonde who held Fatou's lead was just informing her about ponies, and Fatou, after a few seconds of intense reflection, wanted to know if a pony turned into a horse when it grew up. The little blonde laughed and you could see the metal rings of her braces shine.

How old are you? Fatou asked.

Ten, the little blonde responded.

You in fourth grade?

Nope. I'm in fifth. I skipped a grade.

Fatou forced herself to look straight ahead, but I saw her regularly staring at the little blonde like a closed safe.

You an intellectual, she declared, a bit coldly.

Nah, I'm just advanced, that's all! Intellectual means more than that. Intellectual is a disease!

Yeah, well, I know, Fatou hit back with aplomb, *I know!*

I'm scared of horses, I admitted to Alban.

Come on...

I swear.

Scared how?

I can't get on. It's impossible.

What if you had to?

I don't know... I'd tremble? I'd fidget so much that I end up falling? I'd beg to get down? But you know, there are some things in life that you have to do, that you have to go through, but most of the time, no, you're the one who decides. You try. Or not.

Except that it's embarrassing if you don't.

Me, I don't care about that. For this sort of thing, what matters is what happens between you and you.

The little blonde asked Fatou in turn what class she was in. Fatou sank her fingers into the pony's mane and remarked, *Look, it's frizzy.*

WE HAD DRIVEN THE horses back into their stalls and Rodolphe was still looking at me sideways. Forty-five minutes after my fall, the humiliation was still evident in the red in the whites of my eyes, the pink in my cheeks. Flex had brushed Avalanche at top speed, contrary to the others who were pampering their new best friends. Complicity established between fearful human and surly horse, they felt with their fingertips around the nostrils, where the skin is softest, the most supple, murmuring inaudible words of adoration. Flex, however, had sped through the care. As soon as he'd done the bare minimum, he had locked up his stall and come to back me up.

Let him learn to get by on his own! Rodolphe had hissed. *No no, let him do it!* he said to the equestrian center instructor. *No no,* to Flex, who had taken hold of the currycomb and was firmly brushing Diana. *No no,* to Flex again as he lifted the hooves and scraped the mud off with the hoof pick. *You're not helping him,* to Flex, who removed the straps, took off the halter, a makeshift groom. *You don't listen when people're talking to you, like you want a taste of my size nines in your ass,* to Flex who had always had the spirit of someone who'd soon be putting on size elevens, bigger feet than his neighbor. Flex had been born with this essence of rage, dispensed as an example to Rodolphe the powderpuff's face when he came at me with, *Well,* ma pauvre chérie, *do you need a chaperone?* or when, prior to lights-out, lining us up, Rodolphe had asked, for hygiene concerns he claimed, to be sure that we really had taken off our briefs under our pajama pants, *Show me a little cheek*... Flex would pull on the elastic hatefully, *What a giant asshole,* he would whisper, *what a fucking perv*, the pale ceiling lights beating down on our heads, before the burping contest and the midnight snack, fruit jelly stolen away and hidden for four hours in the drawers of our bedside tables, before the games that marked and decorated the confidential world of childhood, temporarily suffocated by the intrusion of a foreign body, this little Rodolphe and his stupid whims, this little cheek that he'd drool over, and which we'd unknowingly expose under his eyes and bad breath.

Bitch, Flex would murmur.

Excuse me? Rodolphe would demand.

Heavy silence in the dormitory.

Nothing, Flex would respond.

That's fine, we can see you've got the strength of your convictions.

Where I would have swallowed my pride and bowed my head, nipped any biting retort in the bud, Flex would raise his voice and say to Rodolphe, loudly and clearly, *Look, all I'm missing when it comes to strength is a foot and a half and some protein. But don't worry, I'm working on it all the time.*

JAIME SÁENZ (1921–1986) is considered the preeminent literary voice of twentieth-century Bolivia. The author of numerous books, Sáenz also conducted "Los Talleres Krupp," late-night salons that precipitated a new generation of Bolivian writers. Sáenz was famously nocturnal, death-obsessed, and bisexual.

Muerte por el tacto

(A modo de manifestarse estupor ante lo bromista de la mirada.)

I

Olvidó los océanos y las voces

replegado con los demás en el apagado símbolo de los puentes—hizo perdurar el crepúsculo

al igual de la condición de los afectos al árbol

los ensangrentados

los de largas cabelleras

los forjadores del viento

los que con la impasibilidad de las cosas han depositado un pétalo

Translated by
TED DODSON

Death at the Very Touch

(In the style of the dumbstruck revealing itself in its own joker of a look.)

I

One forgot the oceans and the voices

—the one who draws out emotion so it lasts as long as the twilight

itself to a tree—refolded under the bridges' muted symbol along with everyone else

those bloodied-up

those long-hairs

those shapers of the wind

those that have, with the utter indifference of very things, deposited a petal

una arena un aire en el arco olvidado de aquella cumbre

los que iniciados en los triunfos de la naturaleza

en las revelaciones de las edades y de las lluvias

anuncian las transformaciones del sonido, figura tuya—no sé aún quién eres

los que sean lo mismo que los ríos parte vital de las montañas

los que sean

los que realmente vivan y mueran sin hacer gesto de desagrado

los que se queden imberbes y también los barbudos y los barrigones

dignos y naturales cuando el sonido y el viento son una misma cosa

cuando no existe necesidad de que no hayan moscas

cuando no se tiene que pagar para que besen a los delegados y el beso ne sea más que beso y no señal torcida hipócrita y atentatoria

cuando el matar no es condenable sino sólo matar y el término con que se designa la acción desaparece

cuando te topes en las esquinas con alguien idéntico a ti y puedas decirle "hola," "ojalá," "tal vez," "recuerda" o "quién sabe"

indistintamente

como si te refirieras a él o a ello o a ellos o a ti desde la luz hacia la luz

es necesario que escriba una carta para poder ver mejor la luz de las cosas

a sand grain, a sky in the forgotten arch of one of those crests

those initiated in nature's ceremonial dance

in the revelations of its age and all its rain

herald the changing key, that note of yours—I still don't know who you are—

those that may be the same as the rivers, a vital part of the mountains

those that seem

those that really live and die without expressing any displeasure

those that stay beardless and the bearded and the beerbellied also

dignified and natural when sound and wind are one and the same

when there's no need for anyone who doesn't have flies all around them

when there's no reason to pay to kiss the delegates and the kiss seeming nothing more than a kiss and not tipping off that it's crooked, hypocritical, and attempted murder

when murder isn't condemnable, only killing and death whose performance is designed to be unseen

when you stumble around a street corner into someone identical to yourself and you might say "hey," "hope so," "every time," "remember," or "who knows"

indistinctly

as if you're referring to him or to it or to them or to yourself, from one light to another light.

luego de leerla alumbrado por el antiguo vuelo de mis amigos muertos

es necesario que recuerden todos su amor a la música, su sosiego y su desdicha,

y su propensión a la risa así como las arquitecturas que urdían cuando podían hacer lo contrario

y su lamento, el lamento que ya fue analizado sin usar la substancia humana,

sin planes, sin palabra ni consulta, pero con ademanes repetidos bajo la mirada

que caía desde un pedestal diseñado en otro tiempo para ensalzar a los mendigos, a los valientes y a los inventores del azúcar y del resorte

y sus proyectos,

los rigurosos alegatos en favor del desquiciamiento, de un anti-orden, para el retorno profundo al verdadero ordenamiento

sus conmovedores argumentos para comprender finalmente el simple significado de la estrella

sus penas tan dignas de respeto

sus venias (te explican el punto de partida de la vida)

encerraban una melodía ingenua y lejana y te inducían a ser más bueno y desentrañar con mayor autoridad los signos misteriosos de las nubes y de las calles

hacían que te vieras tal como eres (tu contenido, las propias venias que jamás harás)

It's necessary to get a better view from the light of very things when I'm trying to write a letter

after reading it lamplit by my dead friends' past departures.

It's necessary everyone remember their love for music, their solitude, and their misery

and their propensity to laugh in just the way architectures might weave together when they could do otherwise

and their lament, a lament that has already been analyzed without human substance

without guidelines, without comment or consultation, but with repeated actions under the watch

that fell from a pedestal used in times past for extolling the penniless, the valiant, and the inventors of sugar and the spring

and their projects

those rigorous allegations in favor of disengagement, of an anti-order supporting a profound return to rightful ordainment

their moving arguments for finally comprehending the simple significance of the stars

their sorrows so worthy of respect

their mercy (making clear to you the starting point of this life)

enclosed a drawn out and naïve melody and incited you to be kinder and to unpack with greater authority the mysterious signs of the clouds and the streets

y les intitulabas medida de todo, y solución secreta de todo, y surgía de tu sombra una venia destinada a ellos

y les intitulabas "caro destino, gayo amigo."

Mi soñoliento cuerpo despierta finalmente, y me hallo frente a mis amigos muertos

y me levanto triste a veces porque de haber un muro a mi frente,

de haber una valla o un duende a mi frente,

yo no estaría triste ni pensaría en ti ni en mí ni en ellos

y es así que salgo encorvado a contemplar el interior de la ciudad y uso del tacto desde mis entrañas oscuras

en el secreto deseo de encontrar allá, allá el medio propicio para hacer que el mundo sea envuelto por el olvido

para que el olvido impere en las primeras máscaras inventadas por la humanidad

para que el olvido sea la fuerza motora y suprema y para que del olvido sólo surja el olvido

¡no puedes tener idea del olvido porque no conoces a mis amigos muertos!

y para que en el curso de las edades el olvido llegue a generar la soledad

para ello habrás de estar presente en aquella estrella

and made it so you can see yourself the way you really are (your contents, your own mercy you'll never show yourself).

You named them "measurement of everything, secret solution of everything," and a mercy endowed to them surfaced from your shadow

and you named them "worthy fate, grinning friend."

My drowsy body finally wakes up, and I find myself in front of my dead friends.

And I get up saddened sometimes because there's a wall in my face

or there's a fence or a demon in my face.

I wouldn't be sad nor would I even think about you or about me or about them.

With that in mind, I set out toward the interior of the city, hunched over in contemplation, and use my darksome entrails to sense my way

in the secret hope of encountering there, there a medium propitious enough to make very things appear enveloped in oblivion

so oblivion presides in the first masks humanity fashioned

so oblivion might be the supreme and driving force and so from oblivion only oblivion surges forth

but you can't hold any idea of oblivion unless you know my dead friends!

And so over the course of ages oblivion comes to form a total solitude

en el rumbo indeciso,

en el caos de la mirada

en modo alguno para determinar, y sí para que se justifique la razón inexorable de lo habido y lo por haber

de modo que lo armonioso sea siempre armonioso, has de estar presente sin poder saberlo

y yo estaré presente y no podré saberlo pero seremos el olvido y la soledad

porque ya hemos sido olvido y soledad cuando nada sabíamos cuando no teníamos la noción de la oreja y del dolor

ni sed

yo te anuncio que sabemos y seremos

harto conocido es el continente de aquel o de aquellos o del que hace cábalas con una jorobita

conocemos a las gentes pero sólo tal cual son y no las sabemos tal cual no son

pese a que carecen de la facultad de no ser porque no saben que pueden no ser o ser

las saben en toda su magnitud mis amigos muertos y yo hablo de ellos con seguridad y orgullo

son mis maestros

el que hayan muerto dice que han existido eternamente antes de que yo existiera

for which you'd need to be present on some star

on an undecided course

by no means readied to be set

in the chaos of its gaze, and if its course is set, its reason is justified as inexorable through anything and everything that once was and will be.

For what is harmonious to remain forever harmonious, you must be present without making it known

and I will be present and I won't know it but we will be oblivion and solitude

because we have already been oblivion and solitude when we knew nothing, when we hadn't even the notion of sound and pain

or thirst.

I yell to you that we know and we are

well known as the continent of this or that or of the one with a slight slouch making mystical premonitions.

We are acquainted with these people but only as they are and we do not know them as they are not

despite their lacking the faculties of nonbeing because they don't know they can be or not be.

My dead friends understand this in all its vastness and I talk to them with confidence and pride.

They are my teachers.

su muerte y sus muertes me enseñan no sólo que puedo ser fabricante de azúcar sino marino, relojero, pintor, físico, geomántico y muchas otras cosas

que puedo tener además desconocidas profesiones y que puedo afectar alegría

coma o no.

Todos han alcanzado un nivel suficiente para descifrar los anhelos que formula aquella lagartija

no se deciden a hacerlo

creen que no hay motivo o no se imaginan creer que haya un motivo

por eso se quedan quietos tocando el tambor

prefieren mirarse a sí

solamente se comunican entre sí
no con lo tenue de las cosas
viven cautamente entre sí
no prefieren alaridos
ni guardan algo en su corazón
para alabar la sombra de aquel zócalo que gime

su congoja no es grande su alegría no es alegría sus manos no son todavía manos parece que sus cabellos no han alcanzado la jerarquía total

decide tú.

One of the dead says they have existed eternally before me.

His death and their deaths teach me that I can be made out of sugar and still be a mariner, watchmaker, painter, physicist, mathematician, and many other things

that I can have additional unfamiliar professions and that I can find happiness

comatose or not.

All of them have reached a plane sufficient for deciphering the yearnings some lizard formulates

but they don't get around to it.

They believe there's no reason to or they can't even imagine believing there's a reason to

so they keep quiet, thrumming on a tambourine.

They prefer to watch each other.

They only communicate with each other
and not with the tenuous nature of very things
they live cautiously with one another
they don't care much for hubbub
nor do they shelter anything in the heart
so they may applaud the shade atop some groaning plinth.

Yo me escondo de las extrañas costumbres—de la actitud con que no se debe resumir una tesis adorable acerca de las cosas sencillas y perfumadas

soy partidario de la lombrices y de los peces
de las estrellas que cantan
guardo devoción por la mirada de los niños
y me gusta dibujar cuando llueve

y cuando se humedecen mis ojos, me es necesario poder hablar el idioma secreto originado durante el triunfo de las cosas

juzgo conveniente alabar la esencia de aquel anciano y detenerme cuando el ayudante de hornero le hace muecas descriptivas

al animal que pasa fugaz ante la sonrisa de la viejecita del dintel

en fin, adoro las voces claras, los trenes y las ciudades

y por todo lo que digo

adoro mis entrañas oscuras.

Their languor isn't great their happiness isn't happiness their hands still aren't hands it seems their hair hasn't made it the total hierarchy

chooses you.

I tuck myself away from these strange customs, from the attitude that maintains an adorable thesis concerning homely and perfumed things shouldn't be summarized.

> I am a partisan of the earthworms and the fishes
> of the stars that sing
> I hold my devotion through the eyes of children
> and I like to draw when it rains

and when my eyes are wetted, I must be able to speak the secret language originated during the ancient dance of the very things.

I judge conveniently to elevate the spirit of the ancients and detain myself when the acolyte of the ovenbird makes dramatic faces

at the animal itself as it passes fleetingly before the smile of the little old lady in the doorway.

In the end, I worship clear voices, the trains and cities

and throughout whatever I say

I worship my darksome entrails.

DAVID ALBAHARI has written novels, short stories, plays, and children's stories. The leading writer of his generation in Serbia, he is also a literary translator. Two collections of short stories and seven novels (including *Checkpoint*) have been published in English translations.

Kontrolni punkt

Sa mesta na kojem smo stajali jasno se videlo zašto je tu postavljen kontrolni punkt—to je bila najviša tačka puta koji se podjednako strmo dizao, odnosno spuštao u odnosu na rampu i kućicu u kojoj su se nalazili rezervni stražari. Iako to nismo nikada proverili i premerili, deo puta koji je vodio uzbrdo bio je, po dužini, jednak delu puta koji je vodio nizbrdo. Ukoliko bi neko krenuo s jedne strane, odozdo, od samog početka, a neko drugi krenuo u isto vreme sa druge strane—uz pretpostavku, dakako, da se svi elementi njihovog hoda podudaraju, odnosno odigravaju na isti način—te dve osobe bi se tačno srele kod rampe. Tačnije rečeno, svaka bi stigla do svoje strane rampe, odakle bi piljila u osobu *iza* rampe. U povratku bi se, pod istim uslovima, naravno, isto desilo, te bi obe osobe istovremeno stupile na ravan deo puta koji se pružao pred njima i onda skretao u šumu. U šumi nismo nikada bili, ne samo zbog toga što to nije bilo predviđeno u okviru našeg zadatka, već i zbog toga što smo svi bili iz grada i šuma nam nije ništa značila. Da je bilo ko od nas ušao u šumu, verovatno ne bi nikada iz nje izašao, izuzimajući Mladena, koji je živeo na nekoj planini. Njemu je šuma bila kao drugi dom i čak bi se moglo pretpostaviti da je naša četa dobila zaduženje da brine o rampi i kontrolnom punktu zahvaljujući Mladenovom poznavanju šumskog bilja. Naime, on je uspešno odgovorio na pitanje čime bi se vojnici hranili kada bi bili primorani da potraže skrovište u šumi. Tako smo stigli ovde i, bar za sada, posle prvih nedelju dana, izgleda da skoro nećemo dobiti novi zadatak. Doduše, to smo sami zaključili jer se za to vreme niko nije pojavio ni sa jedne ni sa druge strane rampe, a radio stanica koja je trebalo da nas povezuje sa komandnim centrom zaćutala je već drugog dana po dolasku i kasnije se oglašavala . . .

Translated by
ELLEN ELIAS-BURSAĆ

Checkpoint

From where we stood, the logic of setting up a checkpoint on this particular spot was clear—this was the highest point on a road that rose and fell just as steeply up to and away from the barrier and sentry hut. Though we never actually measured it, the stretch of road leading uphill was the same in length as the stretch running down. If somebody were to walk from one side, from below, from exactly where the slope began, while somebody else was walking up from the other side at the same time—assuming, of course, that all the elements of their stride were equal and they were moving at the same pace—the two would reach the barrier at the exact same moment. Actually each would arrive simultaneously at their side of the barrier, and from there they'd stare *beyond* the barrier at the other. On their way back, assuming the same givens, of course, the same would occur, in other words both would reach the level part of the road that extended in front of them and ran off into the forest. We never spent time in the forest, not because we'd been told not to but because we were all city kids so the forest meant nothing to us. Had one of us gone into the forest, he probably never would have reappeared, the only exception being Mladen, who'd lived on a mountainside. The forest for him was home sweet home, and it may be that our whole platoon was assigned the task of guarding the barrier and checkpoint because of Mladen's knowledge of forest flora. Apparently he'd given the right answer to the question about what soldiers eat if they're forced to hunker down in the wild. So that's how we ended up here, at least for now, and after the first week it was looking as if we wouldn't be reassigned anytime soon. This was a conclusion we came to on our own because during that first week no one showed up at either side of the barrier and the radio that was supposed to connect us to the command center fell silent the second day after we arrived and would later kick in now and then only at the odd moment. The soldiers didn't dare carry cell phones because of their interference with the military network and none of the three phones the unit had were working as there was no electric power available for recharging. So having no contact with headquarters or the world, we could be said to be as lost as castaways surrounded by boundless expanses of ocean. Worst of all, we had no way of knowing which route we'd taken to get there. The trucks that brought us drove through the night and unloaded us before dawn on the broad path leading through the forest all the way to the checkpoint, and then immediately, while everything around us was still dark, they turned and back they went. When dawn finally broke, no one was sure which road the trucks had used. All around us were tire tracks, of course, but they crisscrossed and overlapped every which way so we couldn't identify the road leading back to home base. It was a few days later that we only began to wonder about this once the unusual quiet of the place had begun to stir our qualms, by which time the tire tracks were barely visible, especially on the grass which had righted since then. We had no choice but to continue doing what we'd come there to do: guard and watch over the passing of people and goods through the checkpoint. To be honest, we hadn't been told whether the checkpoint was on a border lying between two countries or along a line dividing two villages. Perhaps it didn't matter, a soldier's duty, after all, is not to reason why, his is but to obey and only ask questions later, meaning if we'd been told to guard the checkpoint, that's what we'd do and we wouldn't distract ourselves with idle guesswork. So our commander promptly drew up a roster of sentries, cutting back on the number of daytime sentries so the soldiers would be more rested at night, when, for security reasons, there were four on duty. Nothing moved around us by day or night—all the sentries concurred, but our commander, an old-school soldier, had no intention of relenting or reducing the number of sentries on night duty. "Where nothing squeaks," our commander said, "that's where the trouble is brewing." So we guarded a checkpoint where nobody was checked and peered through our binoculars at landscapes through which no one passed. If there was a war still on somewhere, we knew nothing about it. No shots were fired, there was no zinging of bullets, no bomb blasts, no helicopter clatter, nothing. "What if the war's already over," we asked our commander one morning, "shouldn't we be going home?" He was implacable. "We'll go home when they send us home. Until then, here we stay." The soldiers protested, stood there, cried, "Release us, send us home!" The commander did what he could to quiet them but without success. A fractious mob is a fractious mob, whether they're soldiers or civilians, no one listened to the commander so he had to fall back, in the end, on an unappealing but tried-and-true remedy, the pistol. Raising it high above his head he barked that he'd start shooting if they didn't all shut up and return to their posts. A shot was heard. The commander stared, aghast, at his pistol; the shot hadn't come from him but from the gun of one of the sentries who, after we'd assembled by the checkpoint, reported to the commander in a quavering voice that he'd shot when he thought a man in green fatigues had shot first at him. "This is not a thinking matter," barked the commander. "Did he or did he not shoot at you?" "He took aim," said the guard, "but I was faster." The commander sent a group of soldiers to examine the place where the person in the green fatigues had supposedly stood, and off they ran across the meadow. Someone said maybe a bear had devoured a woodsman earlier and everyone burst out laughing. A little later the group of scouts waded back through the brambles. They were holding something green that turned out to be a tatter of ragged fatigues. Nowhere, however, said the scouts, did they find anything to suggest that this filthy, rumpled tatter was what the sentry had seen. Nowhere, they insisted, was there any trace of humans, nothing but paw prints and bird tracks. Did this mean the sentry hadn't seen anything? The commander said nothing. Then he announced the alarm was over and called an assembly. Up we lined and, while the sun warmed our heads from behind, we listened to the commander's warning to remain calm if we wished to grapple with the enemy. True, we knew nothing of who the enemy might be, but once a war is on one speedily acquires both friends and foes. Back we went to our duties—at least those of us who had duties—and our leisure activities, and soon the strains of an accordion could be heard. The cook's helpers brought news of the goulash we'd be served for dinner and there were rumors that there might be cake, which sparked elation among the soldiers and helped them forget how horrific our situation was. The horror showed its ugly face with the commander's order that over the next few days or rather nights, they'd use lights only in cases of the most dire need, and all evening activities such as polishing boots, cleaning weapons, and longer stays outdoors would be reduced to a minimum or switched to daytime. Then smoking came up, which had not been permitted in enclosed areas but only at a distance of ten feet from the building where the men were billeted. We should explain that the checkpoint was not new, nor were the barracks where we were housed, with sleeping quarters, a lecture hall, a bathroom, a mess hall, and a small room for the commander. There were also two latrines near the barracks dating back to whenever, slapped together from unpainted boards and thick with flies and spiders. In one of them, the next morning, a murdered sentry was found. The ones who saw him said he was sitting there, his pants down around his ankles, with a nasty gash across his neck. His gun was propped in the corner, and everything was drenched in blood. When he saw him, the commander cursed with a gasp, spun on his heel, and returned to his office. We stayed outside and spoke in whispers. The sun climbed higher in the sky and the day warmed. Clouds of flies swarmed around the latrine. They hung in the air like clusters of grapes and soon the sentry's entire body began to look more like a black mummy. The commander finally came out, and when he addressed us we could smell the drink on him. He set two men to digging a grave, then other soldiers joined in and soon the grave was ready. "The priest," said the commander, "where's our priest?" He was referring to a soldier who, after three years as a seminary student had transferred to the school of natural sciences and mathematics to study physics and chemistry. The commander dispatched four soldiers to fetch the dead body and soon they returned, toting it on the door they'd pulled off the latrine hinges, and behind them swarmed and quivered the clouds of flies. "Quick," said the commander, "make it quick," the "priest" began mumbling and chanting, the murdered sentry was rolled into the grave, the military-issue shovels scooped in the dirt, and in the time it took to clap two hands together a mound of black and greasy soil piled up before us. Only later did someone think to poke an improvised cross into it, but we never learned who. Nor did we find out who killed him, because after the first rumors of forest avengers lurking in treetops and waiting for us to drop off

We won't just sit here, will we, waiting for someone to stab us, one by one, in the back?

to sleep before creeping in and murdering someone, a question arose, which nobody uttered aloud, but which struck all of us as a genuine possibility: What should we do if it was one of us who'd done him in? We don't know who first raised the question, but afterward it was easy to see how it traveled from soldier to soldier, always scribbling the same astonishment across their faces. In the evening the soldiers tossed and turned for hours, sleepless, chilled by the thought that if the killer were already in their midst they might be next on the list. They dropped off to sleep in the most varied postures, on the floor by the cot, with elbows on the windowsill, by the front door—a cigarette between fingers, until the commander flew into a rage and said he'd ban all smoking. And even if he hadn't blustered as he did, smoking was on its way out. Whoever still had a pack tucked away hid it like a snake hides its legs; as there was no opportunity to stockpile tobacco, the same fate awaited them all. It's easy to imagine that this fear was what pushed the men to talk among themselves about how to make their way back through the forest. We won't just sit here, will we, waiting for someone to stab us, one by one, in the back? They called for the commander to do something and, after conferring with his officers, he ordered the formation of two squads of scouts. The squads were identical, three men each; one (in each squad) carried a light machine gun, while the others were armed with smaller weapons and hand grenades. The squad leaders were also issued flare guns; what with the total lack of communications this would be their only way of signaling their location if they were in crisis. The commander wanted at first to assign Mladen to one of the squads and the soldiers themselves assumed he would, but then the thinking prevailed that Mladen should be kept at the checkpoint in case there was a search for one or both of the scouting squads. And so it was that both squads lined up the next day at dawn by the barrier, one on one side, the other on the other, listened to what the commander had to say, saluted, and marched off down the hill. As we've already said, the distance from the checkpoint to the foot of the hill was almost identical on both stretches of the road and the groups reached the points where the road curved off into the forest at nearly the same moment. Once they were all out of sight, a hush settled over those of us who still stood around the checkpoint. The first to speak was the commander, who asked what there was for dinner, though he knew the answer every bit as well as all the rest of us: mac and cheese, beet salad, and a large chocolate-chip cookie. This was when somebody thought to ask whatever had happened to the tattered scrap of fatigues found in the bushes, did anyone know? "Yes," said the commander, "of course, we examined the uniform, or, I should say: the scrap, since somebody had ripped the uniform to shreds." This was followed by a thorough disquisition on how many tatters there had been, the force required for ripping them, and, ultimately, how there was nothing left to suggest where the uniform had been manufactured and obtained or who had worn it. The only item available to shed some light, though a feeble, rather than a strong, light, was a tarnished token with the number five pressed into both sides. "Such tokens," explained the commander, "are usually used for public telephones or metro rides, but there are no insignia to suggest which city or state uses a token like this one. And perhaps it's no longer in use," continued the commander, "it may be a vestige of some long gone time, a memento, perhaps, which its former owner held on to for years and then forgot in the back pocket of his discarded fatigues. Who knows, he may be searching for it anxiously as we speak, rifling in vain through everything he owns." The soldiers' faces fell and they patted their pockets where they, apparently, carried similar mementos. One soldier asked to inspect the token and it quickly traveled from hand to hand but no one could weigh in about it. There were several arbitrary guesses not worth mentioning. Better, now, a word about the strength of the forces assigned to guard the checkpoint, we've said nothing about this so far, and later there may not be time. So, under him the commander had a cook and a nurse, and three ten-man units, each with a junior officer as leader. The nurse also served as clerk, quartermaster, radio and telegraph operator, and probably even more. No longer, however, could we speak of three ten-man units; the murder of the sentry meant there were two fully manned units and one unit only partially manned. Perhaps the word "murder" was not the best, as there had been no official verdict yet as to cause of death. A few wanted to call the murder a suicide; to do so would

Kerosene lamps and big candles, flames in the night air, created a romantic mood, and who knows what someone might have thought when seeing so many flames flickering in the dark barracks.

relieve the army of responsibility, but in this case that would have been ludicrous. The gash on the right side of his neck could never have been inflicted by the sentry himself, especially as he was right-handed. A suicide would have been easier on the rest of us; there'd have been no need for special caution when we used the latrine. But knowing someone had ambushed him while he was in there groaning and straining to expel his waste, the soldiers began going to the latrine in pairs, sometimes even in a gang of five or six. And while one of them sat inside, the other or others would stand guard. Night, however, posed a problem: no one dared venture out to the latrine in the darkest night, so we prepared a small room to serve as a nighttime toilet. The two, three buckets were carried out as soon as we woke, emptied, and cleaned for the next night. Fortunately, the soldiers were mainly young men, there weren't many who had to slink off to the buckets at night, taking care not to make noise, but nevertheless all soldiers were assigned to the duty of hauling them out and emptying them—not a task they enjoyed, but if everybody was happy all the time there'd be no need for an army, right? The commander was unbending and ready to punish anyone who disrupted the order; he was right there, the next morning, to carry out the first bucket, sloshing with urine and feces, and dump it down the latrine. In the evening, when the daily orders for the next day were read out, he'd announce who was on "sanitation" duty for the next morning, and they were dubbed "shitty granny" or "shitty gramps" by the soldiers. But these nocturnal forays remind us that we need to explain how we managed at all once night fell. First, we had a few kerosene lamps, standard issue for rustic bivouacs, places where there'd probably be only intermittent electric current and other power, and beyond that every soldier was issued a package of slow-burning candles, and there were also plenty of the candles in the squad depot. Kerosene lamps and big candles, flames in the night air, created a romantic mood, and who knows what someone might have thought when seeing so many flames flickering in the dark barracks. More eyes may have been watching than we knew. Hence the difference between us and "them": they always knew more about us than we about them, especially when it came to numbers. Whatever the case, the next morning we found a dead raven. One of its legs had been crushed, its wings snapped, its beak plucked out. The soldiers pressed around it, shouted, and cursed. They were more unsettled by the dead bird than by the latrine sentry murder. "Whoever they are they're not human," said one soldier, "they're monsters and they deserve to die!" "Now!" shouted other soldiers and gathered around the commander when he came over to see what was up. They pointed to the raven, but apparently the commander was not as alarmed; he told them to pull themselves together. "Our men are out in the forest," said the commander, "and until they return, no one moves, understand?" The soldiers mumbled something conciliatory and returned to their duties. The sun beat down mercilessly, most unusual for the time of year, and some of the soldiers quickly tanned to a bronze, but there were others whose backs, arms, and shoulders, and, I should add, faces, became a mass of blisters. "We won't be sleeping tonight," thought the commander, but then the cry went up: "Here they are, they're coming!" When the commander ran over to the checkpoint there they were: the squads had apparently each lost one man. In each, two of the soldiers were carrying the third. They toiled up the hillside so we, while they were still far away, could hear their labored breathing and choked coughs. Each squad reached the barrier at almost exactly the same moment and a person remarked that somehow, somewhere in the forest, each must have taken a wrong turn: each returned to the same side of the checkpoint from which they'd left. But when the men were told, they insisted doggedly that they could not remember one path intersecting another nor that they were ever in doubt about which way to go. "The forest was hushed," said one of the soldiers, "and we took care to honor the quiet. Had we run into the other squad, our conversation would have sent out shockwaves like a bomb blast." This may explain why both soldiers were killed by arrows, an old-fashioned yet deadly weapon, the fletching still protruding from their chests. The commander fumed and swore up a storm, using curses even the worst drunks and bastards would have been proud of, though, obviously, nobody could blame him. Everything might have been different had we known why we were there, what we were protecting, from whom. What could possibly have been the point of a checkpoint on a road that no one ever traveled which may have run in a circle? Or was its sole goal an illusion of passage, a chimera of progress, a launching pad for new victories yet a trap, bait for the gullible, a carbon monoxide van to swallow souls, inside which people died from a surfeit—not a shortage—of air? Or, as one soldier put it, everything is so unreal exactly so we won't figure out that "our side" was actually attacking us, unaware, perhaps, that we're "theirs." Who is "our side" in this war, anyway, where we're making this guest appearance, where even we have no idea what we're up to here? Wouldn't it make more sense for us to march home and put this all behind us? No, no, and no, scowled the commander, there will be no homeward march. And besides, he asked, where would we march to, and how—does anyone know? The telephone lines are down, the radios dead, we have no carrier pigeons to fly our messages out, and even if someone were to set out for the headquarters, which road should they take to get there? Is there such a road? The commander summoned the clerk and issued his order for the next day: we were to spend the whole day searching for a solution to our outlandish predicament. We owe this to those who've died, announced the commander during our modest repast: a big roll and a small tin of sardines for each. During dinner something else happened, a story flew from ear to ear that men from one of the squads, only two, had caught sight of village dwellings in the distance through a haze across a clearing. One of them even swore he heard cows mooing and dogs barking. It was still early, wisps of fog swirled among the trees and over the meadows, but from the chimneys of the houses rose puffs of smoke, the household was up and about, probably at breakfast, and they'd soon be going out to tend to their morning duties. The soldiers, the two, even saw a front door slowly open, but then the order came to move on and off they went. They quickly told the squad leader and he heard them out but wouldn't go back. That, he said, as the two soldiers reported, would give the advantage to whoever was following them, and there definitely were people, sad to say, who were after them to ambush them without mercy. The commander heard the rumors and called the two men over. He asked the corporal who'd escorted them to step away because he didn't want any part of their conversation to be leaked. He questioned the soldiers closely about the houses and farmyards they'd seen, and he even sketched a house with a few quick strokes to see if it resembled what they'd seen, despite or because of the fog, which had drawn them with its swirls. Once the soldiers had told him what they knew, the commander, as they later said, took from a drawer a map that had been folded and refolded many times, smoothed it out, placed a compass on the table, and gauged something for a few minutes with a compass and a protractor. Of course he might be mistaken, but if we gave him the benefit of the doubt, he said, then where those two soldiers said they'd seen houses and outbuildings—there was nothing, or, and now this really was strange, said the commander, there once had been houses like the ones they described, but—here he stopped and stared away into the distance—the whole area had been flooded a little farther north to make a reservoir for a hydroelectric dam that was never, said the commander, put into operation. Are you sure, he asked, now standing in front of the entire company, that the houses you saw weren't under water? But the soldiers were quick to dismiss this idea, or that what they'd seen might be a mirage. Both laughed aloud as if they'd spent a whole evening rehearsing this in tandem. Someone said, "Let Mladen have a look," and they all hastened to concur. Mladen knew how to survive in the forest, so he'd know where to look and what to see. A spat later flared about whether he should go alone or with an escort, but the commander interrupted this as it ended—or almost ended—saying we were out of time. A person alone is always more efficient than two or three. "In the old days, many an expedition floundered," said the commander, "because the leader would have to keep track of an oversized crew: cooks, dog handlers, natives, masseuses." Then he suggested we ask Mladen whether he needed an escort. As far as he was concerned, said Mladen, an assistant might be helpful, but he was better off on his own. He'd be speedier and more effective, with no worries about what to do if his assistant were hit or, god forbid, killed, or, worse yet, captured and interned. Well then, said the commander, get ready and off you go. The sooner we know the truth about the houses and village, the sooner we can wrap this up. But a few soldiers noticed discrepancies between what the commander said before and his sudden tale of a power plant, and all this while waving the mystery map. Where had it come from is what the soldiers and others wanted to know. If he was their commander, he couldn't be oblivious one minute, and then all talk the next like some history expert. Then they all clammed up because Mladen appeared. Though nightfall was still hours away, he'd smeared his face with black paint; nothing gives a person away, he said, like moonlight lighting up your face. Several soldiers came over to plead with him to take them along. Mladen urged them to go to the commander but they refused. One said he'd go with Mladen no matter what. "They'll shoot you between the eyes," said

If animals were treated this way, wondered Mladen, what had happened to the people?

Mladen, pointing at the soldier's forehead and pulling an imaginary trigger. "I am going, too," said the soldier, raced off to pack, and no one ever saw him again. His disappearance was only noticed later when Mladen came back and asked what had happened to the pushy soldier who'd wanted to go with him no matter what. He'd thought of the man, said Mladen, when he sank into quicksand and tried to wriggle free without losing his boots and weapons. He'd have given anything just then to have the young man along so he could reach out with a branch, but since the soldier wasn't there, Mladen struggled on his own. Luckily, he was mired in a shallows, or whatever they're called, and bit by bit, inch by inch, he squirmed out onto solid, grassy turf. He lifted first one foot and then the other so we could see the mud caked to his boots. It took him only one night to reach the spot the two soldiers had described, but he stayed there till daybreak to corroborate their story. Ah ha, said the commander, what did he see? He saw the house, like the soldiers said, but no smoke puffing from the chimney and the front door was not even open a crack. A window was open and curtains swayed in gusts of wind. He waited, said Mladen, till the sun climbed high in the sky but nobody appeared, not a soul stepped out of the house, not a farm animal left the barn. Just when he thought it was time to come back, he noticed a duck followed by an orderly trail of ducklings. The duck waddled over to the front door and Mladen could see it lift its beak; it was probably summoning someone, the person who, he assumed, regularly came out to feed them. But the water? asked the commander. The water and the lake? No water, no lake, said Mladen, just carnage. The duck was quacking to someone and this is what persuaded him to venture out to see. No path led there, or he hadn't yet found it, so Mladen scrambled down a steep slope from the meadow, stepped across a ravine over a little brook, probably a raging torrent in the spring and summer rains, spilling over its narrow streambed. Hence the quicksand into which he'd so infamously plunged. That's when he mentioned the soldier who'd wanted to tag along and only then did we realize the soldier was missing. The commander wrung his hands and sobbed with a woman's breathy gasps, and then he pulled himself together and said he'd organize a search party and comb the terrain. Absolutely not, said Mladen, too late now, anyway. If he's alive, he's too far off to hear us, and if he's dead, all we can do is build him a monument. Forget it, called one of the soldiers, tell us what happened at the house! First he came across a dog that had been gutted, Mladen told us, then he saw a cat with its spine broken, and in the barn he found two dead cows and a crazed horse. If animals were treated this way, wondered Mladen, what had happened to the people? He thought it was time to go back, his assignment was only to see whether the houses did, in fact, exist, and not to find out what happened to the people who'd been living there. Then he heard groaning and forgot everything else. He hopped over a twisted fence, approached slowly the side of a building, and looked into the backyard. There he saw a ghastly scene: on a large wooden table lay two bodies: an older man, already dead, and an older woman, still alive and moaning in pain. Their bellies were slashed side to side, partly disemboweled, intestines dangling off the table. Mladen turned, he said, and when he went into the house he found the rest of the family: two young men, a woman, and a little girl. They had all, apparently, been raped and strangled or shot dead with a bullet to the head. Nothing in the house was touched, as if the marauders had taken care to be tidy. Judging by the few flies and no stench, Mladen figured the massacre must have happened the night before, and this made him especially cautious; he gave up looking further at other houses. And besides, he said, he didn't know whose side the victims were on, and who the murderers were fighting for. He'd called them murderers, he said, because if he were to call the people who'd perpetrated the atrocities by any other name, or referred to them as soldiers, he'd be insulting all those who'd respected treaties and conventions in wars. And nothing he'd seen hinted at who the perpetrators might be? asked the commander. The soldiers howled, saying they didn't even know whom they were up against. Maybe, said the soldiers, they were a buffer force sent to a conflict near their country's border, though maybe, said others, this is actually a civil war and they, as an official armed force, were dispassionately helping to subdue the conflicts. The commander stood, waited for the soldiers to quiet down, and then said he wished he could explain things to them, but he, too,

The commander looked like someone always on the verge of tears, but though we found this disturbing we didn't know how to help. Is the forest enchanted? mused someone. Is what we think to be happening nothing but an illusion?

was in the dark. In the old days, he said, this happened often; the kingdoms were vast and heralds had to travel for days to bring news to distant provinces of the end of a war. In the Second World War on the little islands scattered across the Pacific there were Japanese fighters who thought the war was still on for decades and they'd shoot at every American who came near. Our situation is not as bad as all that, said the commander, though our ignorance is appalling, but what could he do, he asked, when he was woken that night, as we were? He'd barely had time to pull on his uniform and rush downstairs to the jeep waiting for him out in front. At the assembly point they'd said everything would be explained over the radio; the trucks were ready and required the cover of darkness. Well sure, recalled the commander, he'd been handed an envelope with a map, the rosters of fighters, and lists of issued weapons and equipment. The lists were full of errors, said the commander, so he'd already made his own list of the things missing from the lists. The map was no good or out-of-date as we could see from Mladen's report and the stories of the soldiers who'd seen the house, where, according to the commander's map, there was supposed to be a reservoir. The commander looked like someone always on the verge of tears, but though we found this disturbing we didn't know how to help. Is the forest enchanted? mused someone. Is what we think to be happening nothing but an illusion? Who believes in magic? asked others, though no one could gainsay the possibility that hallucinogens had been used, but narcotics can't replace a magic wand, this we knew. Ever since our arrival, said the commander, he'd been doing nothing but juggling lists and making new ones. They're rife with errors, said the commander, not just the lists, the world. Wherever we go we'll find errors, most of all when they insist there aren't any. What he'd like, said the commander, was that there be no errors in the new roster he started yesterday, and he'd like that roster to stay brief, he sincerely hoped it would though he knew that no one, except just maybe He who was on high—here he stopped and raised his eyes to the heavens and all of us looked upward after him—knows in advance just how long that roster will be. All of us, of course, understood what roster he had in mind, just as we all knew it held, so far, four names: the sentry killed in the latrine, the two men shot by arrows while patrolling the forest, and, finally, the soldier who set out on his own after Mladen. A hush. We were prepared to honor the victims of a war which, like every war, is pointless, but each of us was also hoping the next name wouldn't be ours. We said nothing and darted dirty looks at each other as if we were sworn enemies, but what else can you think of someone who hopes to see you dead? "I don't want to die," blurted one of us and we all burst out laughing, not that we were laughing at death, but with relief at the thought that all of us felt the same way.

特集 日本の新鋭詩集

The Japanese Vanguard

Introduction

A vanguard is at the forefront of its field, and what we see from this selection of poetry is that this vanguard is a thoughtful, cautious group. These poems have beauty and levity, but what ties them together is a sense of wariness, ranging from plaintive meanderings to stark predictions. Here are six young poets who have not been widely translated into English and who are working against the grain. Their watchfulness takes on a tone at times philosophical, at times frantic. Jeffrey Angles's translation of Ōsaki Sayaka's "Slowly Flowing Particles of the World" is a chronicle of what people don't notice, until:

> Almost everyone saw something
> Almost everyone overlooked something
> One by one, the invisible was transformed into words

Words we continue to either notice or ignore. Wagō Ryōichi, also translated by Jeffrey Angles, considers the implication of words he cannot ignore:

> "forty years until the reactor is decommissioned" (at present)
> but in my language
> how many years will it take
> to replace the word *reactor*
> with *decommissioned reactor*

A vanguard exists to experiment and push boundaries, but we're reminded that it can also raise the alarm. As we go through our world, with so much available to observe and overlook, Ken'ichi Sasō, translated by Noriko Hara and Joe DeLong, warns us:

> The visible becomes the commonplace.
> The illuminated becomes the commonplace.
> We forget it—
> the irreplaceable.

EMILY WOLAHAN

HACHIKAI MIMI (born in 1974) publishes poetry, stories, essays, reviews, and translations. Her latest collection, *Kao o arau mizu* (2015), is highly praised for its private, yet palpable language that addresses the present and recollects transcendental human experiences.

さまよう庭をさまよう

砂に似た色をひろげる
どこまでも、ひろがっていく
庭を見つけようと思う
　見出そうと、
　　あぶり出そうと、
　　　あるいは、見つけながら手放そう、

そう思う　砂に似た色、
ベージュを　どこまでもひろげて
わたしはそこに　もののかたちを
流してみる　あぶり出してみる
見出して　みる
　くろいかけら、あれはなんだろう
　　あおいかけら、あれは
　　　しろいかけら、あれは蝶、紋白蝶
　　　　はなびら、満開の、
　　　あるいは枯れようとする、つぼみ
　　深緑の葉っぱ、黄緑の、枝、小枝

すべてのはじまりの色
そんなものはなくても、

Translated by
KYOKO YOSHIDA

Wandering the Garden of Wandering

I will find a garden
That spreads the sand-like color
Spreading boundlessly
    I will discover,
        I will unveil,
          or I will find while letting it go

So I will   the sand-like color
Spreading boundlessly   the beige
I will try to shed   unveil
Discover   and see
Shapes and figures
    a piece of black, what is that
        a piece of blue, that is
          a piece of white, that is a butterfly, a small cabbage white
            petals in full bloom,
          or withering buds
        leaves in deep green, branches, twigs, in yellowish green

決めなければならない瞬間
そんなものはあって、
どこからやって来るのだか
ふと訪れる色という色は　息を殺して
投げ出すもの投げ出してまざりあう

かたちを求めてかたちにならないもの
なることを拒むもの
いまにも　かたちになろうとするものや
ならなくてもいっこうに構わないもの
ほどいて　溶けゆく　飛びたつ
　沈みこむ　ふりむく
　　ひそめる息、影
ひとつひとつに影また影

〈ここはどこ?〉
〈庭、かもしれない〉
〈どこの?　いつの?〉
〈どこにもない庭、どこにでも、ある庭〉
〈なにが見える?〉
〈見えるものは、見たいもの〉

この、砂に似た色の、

まざりあう流れにかたちを結んで
そうしてなにかを始め
仮の終わりを目撃し
細胞は入れ替わっていく刻々と
さまよう庭　それはいま
このまぶしさに運ばれていく

While there is no such thing as
The color of all beginnings,
There is such thing as
The moment of decision,
Where do they come from
They come suddenly color after color   holding their breath
They abandon what they abandon and fuse

What remain shapeless in pursuit of shapes
What refuse to take shape
What is about to take shape   at any moment
And what need not to take shape at all
unravel   melt in   fly away
sink in   turn around
hushed breaths, shadows
one by one and shadow after shadow
<Where am I?>
<A garden, perhaps>
<Where? When?>
<A garden of nowhere, a garden of—anywhere>
<What do you see?>
<What you see is—what you want to see>

These, the sand-like colors,
Where they join the stream, shapes emerge
And set something going
Witnessing a transient end
Cells replace one another minute by minute
A wandering garden   here and now
Carried away by this radiance

Translated by Kyoko Yoshida

食うものは食われる夜

音たてちゃ　いけない　今夜は
もの音たてちゃ　いけない
背をあわせ　うつろの胴は長くして
横たわる　濡れた眼玉に
すがた映し合い寝たりは　しない
背をあわせ　川音高く　聞き耳たてる
しない夜はなにも　させもしない夜で
音たてちゃ　いけない　今宵は
もの音たてちゃ　いけない
燃え落ちる魂つぎつぎとななめに光り
液体の法則にどこまでも抗い　呼んで
鱗　はげ落ち　岩肌　はりつき
川底から伸びあがるもの根こそぎ抜かれ
抜かれたものたち　押し流されて
小石の身震い　影の後追い　鰓呼吸
あかあかと　のぼるかれらに
沈黙の判例を　迷わず捧げ
声を忍んで　月に刺されて
くるまれている夜着のうち

Those Who Eat Are Eaten Tonight

don’t make   any noise   tonight
do not make   any noise
pressed against one another’s back   hollow belly stretched
they lie down   they dare not
sleep reflecting one another   upon their wet eyeballs
pressed against one another’s back   over the loud torrent   they listen
the night they do not   is the night they let not
don’t make   any noise   this evening
do not make   any noise
fireball souls sparkle falling across one after another
resisting the laws of fluid to the end   they call
scales flake off   clung to the rock
those reaching from the river bottom uprooted altogether
those uprooted   are washed away
pebbles trembling   shadows following   aquatic respiration
burning red   they climb forward
a silent precedent   offered without hesitation
suppressing our voice   pierced by the moon
muffled in our bedclothes

if you hear this, you will die
what is *this*?
king salmons   queen salmons   running now

Translated by Kyoko Yoshida

これを聴いたらしんでしまう
これってなあに
おおすけ　こすけ　いまのぼる

忘れはしない　のぼってくる
呼吸を合わせ川床すりつつ上ってくる
みずのにおいは鱗の奈落へ染み渡り
内側から叩きのめすそのとき
中心に移ってくるひとつの考え
足を取るあおじろい回遊すべては
今宵のため　むすばれてきたと
川瀬に寄せられ　息　できない
しらないひとに　のしかかられて
言おうとする下にも　知らないひと
いうことが　あるんだけれども
飲みこむしかなく　集めない鰓に
遠ざけられ　殖えていく
満たされたのち　消えていく
積まれる仕草は　いつか寝耳に
そそぎこまれたものに　近い
鱗におおわれた音におおわれ
川明かり　余すところなく飲みくだし
河原と　人の家　押し包む

これ聴いたらしんでしまう
これって　なに
おおすけ　こすけ　いま　とおる
音たてちゃ　いけない　今夜は
もの音たてちゃ
いけない

remember   they are running up
breath against breath they are running up sliding along the riverbed
the water's smell infiltrate into the abyss of scales
beating up from inside and that moment
one thought moves to the center
all the pale migration carrying them away
is for this evening   they've come being united
washed to the shallows   breathless
pressed against   by strangers on top
trying to address   other strangers underneath
though they have   something to say
only to swallow it   distanced
by the gills that gather nothing   they spawn
after fulfilled   they expire
their piling gestures   similar to
something that was poured into   the dreaming ear
covered with the sound that is covered with scales
in the river gleam   nothing left to swallow down
shroud   riverbanks   and houses

if you hear this, you will die
what is *this*?
king salmons   queen salmons   now   passing
don't make   any noise   tonight
do not make
any noise

Translated by Kyoko Yoshida

二重の欲望

海胆（うに）をたべない国から　三日の出張　その人のとなりに
隙間のないふり添って立ち　ながめる先へ海胆の集まり
食用でなくても　おいしそう　水族館　人工の　磯遊び
暗い水輪のみなもとへ　寄せて　返して　落ちるもの
割り切られた場所に　転がる大小　起きているのか
ねむっているのか　わからない　起きているのが六なら
眠っているのは十五　蛍光燈　浴びるとき　息して
打ち消しの波は　遅れに遅れ　追いかけて　今度こそ
はっきりと　おいしそう　触れていい　そう書いてある
ここのひとが勝手に　決めている　海胆には聞かずに
つまみ上げ　濡れたまま　黒く手に受け　手を濡らし
中心を　重たく湿らせ　たべられることなく　この先も
さわられるだけさわられていくやつに　息　吹きかける
海胆を口にしない国の人　おとなしい鼻先へ　近寄せて
栗みたい　だいじょうぶなのさわっても　あぶないね
よりいっそう　おいしそう　干からび切る寸前
水へ放れば　後ろから覗いたよそのひとが　突然
たべられるんじゃないの　それ　そのままで　生で

Doubled Desire

from the country that doesn't eat sea urchin   on a three-day business trip   the man's side
I stand by pretending there's no room left   our gaze ends at a huddle of sea urchins
edible or inedible   looking delicious   the aquarium   its artificial   tide pool
toward the source of the dark ripples   they comb   backwash and drop
in the space cut and divided   big and small ones sit around   whether they're awake
or asleep   remains unknown   if six are awake
fifteen are asleep   flooded with   fluorescent lights   when they breathe
the erasing beachcomber   comes too late   this time around   I chase
clearly   looking delicious   you may touch them   so it says
it's been decided   at the whim of the staff   without asking the sea urchins
I pinch one up   still wet   blackly on my palm   wetting my palm
its center   heavily moist   I blow   a breath into
the little guy we fondle all we want   will never be eaten   forevermore
the man from the country that doesn't smack at sea urchin

Translated by Kyoko Yoshida

閉めたばかりの蓋　跳ね上がり　隠した流れ　暴かれる
そうか　たべるんですねこの国では　黙ることが亀裂を
ふたりのあいだへ　しずかに引いて　中身ですか　そう
割って中身を　醤油つけてね　食べ方まで表へ押し出す
笑みの背に　鋭く羽ばたくもの見えて　浮き足みえて
そう　脇向けばもう　澄んだ別の水槽へ　移ったあと
消滅が立ちこめ　触れたのは　どれ　同類にまぎれて
探せない　あれかな　荒磯(ありそ)の岩陰　身をかがめ　ひとの
におい払おうとしている　あれかな　身の底から光って

to his docile nozzle I reach out
it's like a chestnut is it all right to touch it looks dangerous
looking delicious all the more so just short of shriveling
I toss it back to the water then a stranger peeks from behind
out of the blue
you can eat it can't you au naturel as it is this thing

the lid I've just shut flips up the hidden current
gets exposed
ah I see so you eat it in this country the silence draws
a crack quietly between the two its insides? yes insides
crack it open and dip it in soy sauce I even let out the way we
eat it
on the back of his smile I see something flapping sharply
I see his tiptoeing
yes long before I turn to the side has he moved to
another limpid fishtank
saturated with disappearance which one is the one I touched
mingled among its likes
can't find it is that the one in the shade of the rocky shore
shrinking itself to wash
off the human tang is that the one glowing from its bottom

詩

Born in 1968, KEN'ICHI SASŌ is the author of eight books of poetry. The poems in this issue are from his collection *The Forest That Sounds Like Waves*, in which he explores the connection between the natural world and human experience, both individual and collective.

月食

影を重ねるのだ
疎外された光を鎮めて
撫でていくのだ

小さくなりがちの
生に
宇宙が迫る

●●●●●

三日月だったり満月だったり
そのような
夜々の心のかたち

大きなひろがりを仰ぐなら
闇は漂白されていく

見えない時も
つかずはなれず
青空のかなしみの彼方でも
うっすらと見守るもの

時の紫外線に耐えながら
熱に焼かれて傷を負った後

Translated by
NORIKO HARA AND JOE DELONG

Lunar Eclipse

Shadows have piled upon one another.
Quelling an alienated light,
they have a soft caress.

It is to this life that tends
to become small
that the universe draws closer.

●●●●●

Like alternating between a crescent moon and a full moon—
every night
the heart assumes a certain shape.

If we look up toward the great expanse,
that darkness will be bleached.

Even when it's invisible,
it remains at a reasonable distance.
Even in the great yonder of the blue sky's sadness,
it is something dim to gaze at.

While putting up with time's ultraviolet rays,
after being burnt by the heat and suffering a wound,

詩

海原に心の波を引き起こす
異界の引力

他から我が身に照らされる光ごと
闇にいる他者を照らす
そのような存在

●●●●●

着陸したそこが灰色のでこぼこであっても
夢のかけらもなかったと
宇宙飛行士は言わなかった

うさぎはもう彼方にいないから
現代のかぐや姫は第三惑星にとどまるけれど
人為的に汚されていくこの闇を
照らし続ける

●●●●●

夜の幕に包み込み
ゆっくりと
夢を回していく

そのように
内なる月食

尽くされるものから
尽くすものへ

影の舞踏の愛撫

＜いつもありがとう＞

in the deep ocean, the heart's waves are induced.
The gravity from a world other than our own.

From within others, each light illuminating me
also shines on someone in the darkness.
That kind of existence.

●●●●●

Even though there were gray bumps where they landed,
and the shards of dreams weren't there,
the astronauts didn't mention it.

Because the rabbit isn't on the moon either,
the modern day Princess Kaguya remains on the third planet, but
this artificially polluted darkness
continues to shine.

●●●●●

Enveloped by night's curtain,
we leisurely
cycle through dreams.

In that way,
the lunar eclipse unfolds inside us.

From those for whom efforts were made
to those making efforts.

The intimacy of the shadow's dance.

"As always, thank you."

Translated by Noriko Hara and Joe DeLong

見えることがあたりまえになって
照らされることがあたりまえになって
忘れてしまう
かけがえのないもの

薄明かりに
道の行方を信じることは
時代遅れなんかじゃない

闇を恐れず
歩き続けることだ

●●●●●

むき出しの時代の熱にさらされて
愚かな国の
さびしい秋の夜
小さいまちの
橋で、道で、ベランダで、境内で
月と地球のラブシーンを見つめる人びとの
祈りの影が
そっと
発光している

The visible becomes the commonplace.
The illuminated becomes the commonplace.
We forget it—
the irreplaceable.

In twilight
believing in the ways of your whereabouts
is never passé.

It's a matter of not fearing the dark
and continuing to walk.

●●●●●

Bleached by the bare heat of this era.
A lonely autumn night
of a foolish nation.
On a small town's
bridge, road, veranda, and temple grounds—
people staring at the moon and earth's love scene—
the shadow of their prayers
softly
radiates across the face of the earth.

詩

生きているのです

生きているのです
血まみれの遺体を見せられても
現場が確認されても
生きているのです

報復するって
誰にするのですか
直接殺した人を殺しますか
土地の人びとを空爆しますか
これを機に軍事を加速させますか

誰に報復しても
この生命は
帰ってきません

でも生きています
生きているのです

取材の方々
どうして目が輝いているのですか
お金は弾むからと
いつまで不幸を撮影するのですか

世界は願いでできていると
信じ続けていいですか

Truly Alive

He is truly alive.
Even if we're forced to view a bloody corpse
or confirm a crime scene,
he is truly alive.

They say you'll take your revenge.
On whom?
Will you kill those directly responsible for killing?
Will you bomb the locals?
Taking advantage of this opportunity, will you accelerate military affairs?

No matter whom you took your revenge on,
life
would never come back.

However, he is alive.
Truly so.

Reporters—
why do your eyes sparkle?
You pay the money out.
How long will you keep recording sorrow?

Would it be all right to continue believing
the world is made of our wishes?

Translated by Noriko Hara and Joe DeLong

心臓が止まりました
口がふさがれました

だから

引き継ぐのです
願いの鼓動を
夢の語りを

生きている限り

His heart stopped.
His mouth closed.

So

I will inherit
the beat of our wishes,
the narrative of our dreams.

As long as I am alive.

輪っか

買う人＜買えないなあ＞
売る人＜売れないなあ＞
働く人＜苦しいなあ＞
納める人＜払えないなあ＞
買う人＜買えないなあ＞
売る人＜売れないなあ＞
働く人＜苦しいなあ＞
納める人＜払えないなあ＞

なんという輪っか！

目が回るなんてもんじゃない

ニュースに揺れる満員電車
つり革が首つりに見えてきて

駅前カードローン看板タレントが笑っている
リッチライフ、ワンダフルライフ

霞みが好きだと財力の密会に
原子力オトモダチ作戦だってある

踊らされるぐるぐる
さびついた輪っかは追い詰められて

＜あした＞を確定申告できるだろうか

Circle

Buyer: "Oh, I cannot buy."
Seller: "Oh, I cannot sell."
Worker: "Oh, I'm in poverty."
Payer: "Oh, I cannot pay."
Buyer: "Oh, I cannot buy."
Seller: "Oh, I cannot sell."
Worker: "Oh, I'm in poverty."
Payer: "Oh, I cannot pay."

What a circle!

Much worse than just dizziness.

On a jam-packed train thrown into confusion by news,
a strap starts looking like a suicide by hanging.

Celebrities smile on billboards for credit cards.
Rich life, wonderful life.

If you like the haze, Kasumi, you can join a secret meeting with
    financial power
and even nuclear energy *friendship* operations.

Forced to dance around,
the rusty circle is driven into a corner.

Can it file a final income tax return of "tomorrow"?

Translated by Noriko Hara and Joe DeLong

詩

ENOMOTO SACLACO (born in 1987) occupies a fundamentally oppositional stance toward Japanese literature and society as a whole. Her experimental work comprises a structurally and semantically dense prose poetry said to be nearly unreadable. She is also openly transsexual and willing to speak publicly on this and other taboo subjects.

ANADYOMENE

海の泡、
その映像を念写すること、
あまりに林檎らしい時間、
首をくねらせて踊る、
跳躍する蝗の花々、
それを灰黒い布で覆って、
筋肉の普遍的な動作を、
眺める、
小さな球根が、
脚を伸ばして、
髭を剃る、
角砂糖をひとつからませて、
電飾を巻きつけると、
虚ろな未亡人の曇った目を翳める不純な黄鉄鉱、
になれる、
かもしれない、
だから蓋から卵の殻を無数にとりだし、
しろく濁った湧き水に浸してしまえば、
横から、
毛糸玉の、
胡桃のような臓器を手にした、
毛糸玉の走る音だけが、
摩擦、

Anadyomene

The ocean's foam
To project its image with psychic photography
A time too much like apples
Wiggling the neck around and dancing
Locust flowers prancing about
Cover them with an ash black cloth
And gaze upon
The universal movement of the muscles
The small bulb
Stretches its legs
And shaves its beard
Implicated (entangled) by one sugar cube
Wrap it up in decorative illumination, then
Maybe
You can become
Impure yellow steel that dims the eyesight of the hollow widow with
    cloudy eyes
That's why you pull out countless eggshells from the cover
And when you dip them in cloudy-white spring water
From off to the side
Someone holds an internal organ in their hand
Like a walnut or a ball of yarn
Only the sound of the ball of yarn running

噴きだしているのだ、
そういうこども、
喉の奥から、
鄙びた檜の枝葉、
生やして、
目、
を瞑る、
たぶん嘘だと錯覚してしまうほど、
魚の鱗で満たされた循環、
庭、
転がるように桟敷、
ひろげて、
おおきく重なりあった鍵盤を、
呪術、
奪いとってしまえば、
すべては完了する、
しないかもしれないことを考慮する、
鈴のなかの乳歯、
石臼に挽かれた平らな馬が、
涎を尻ごみさせている、
丁寧に壜詰めにされたぼうふらみたいな人々、
乱暴な北から膨らんでくる蛭、
牛刀の柄を握る達磨は、
石鹸を口から溢れさせている、
だからこそ蝶番が必要なのだ、
二枚貝を閉じたり開いたりするためには、
もちろん枯れ草に足をとられて、
額をしたたか打ったり、
穏やかな風を孕んだ、
波のような至福を、
島、
島影にまつわる赤銅、
捩じれてばかり、
乳房はこぼれ落ち、

And friction or rubbing
Then spurting out
That kind of child
From the back of the throat
Branches of rustic Japanese cypress
Growing
The eyes
Closed
The cycle filled with so many fish scales
You'd be deluded into thinking it must be a lie
A garden
As if rolling around the dress circle
Which is extended
Hugely overlapping keyboards
Magic
If you take them by force
It'll all be over (perfect)
But considering the fact that it might not be
Milk teeth in a bell
A flat horse ground in a stone mortar
Recoils from the drooling
People like mosquito larvae carefully bottled
Leeches swelling as they come from the boisterous north
A Dharma doll holding a butcher knife
Soap overflows from its mouth
That's why you need hinges
In order to open or close a clam
Since of course you'll lose your footing on the dry grass
Beating the forehead
Impregnating a gentle breeze
Supreme bliss like waves
An island
Bronze surrounding its outline
Always getting all twisted up

割れた欠陥だらけの、
石膏像、
金星から火星へ虹が架かっている、
渡る理由もないし、
火山帯、
鍛冶屋の金床を叩く、
嫉妬の気配、
積乱雲に包まれた、
浅い海底からの閃きの構造、
象牙質の紐が靡いて、
たなびいて、
雛菊を背中に生やして、
風に戦がせている、
それは鉤針に襲われた汚れかもしれない、
鹿の蹄のかたちが残っている、
金箔がはらはらと舞い落ち、
赤い珊瑚の音、
雑木林の饒舌さに堆く盛られた、
石塔、
溺れる空気の吐いた、
悲鳴が滲んで、
沈着していく枯葉の儚さ、
滑らかに、
傾いて、
なだらかな畦道を思い浮かべながら、
その三叉路をじっと、
吊るされたように、
侍らせて、
焦がれた茅葺き、
湯気がいつまでも屯している、
滞りなく、
つつがなく、
枕木のうえを跨ぐ名前のわからないものの声、
禊の雪に覆われて、

The breasts spill over and fall
Cracked and full of defects
The plaster figure
A rainbow hangs suspended from Venus to Mars
But there's no reason to cross
And besides, the volcanic belt
Strikes the blacksmith's anvil
Signs of jealousy
Wrapped in a thundercloud
The structure of a flash of insight from the shallow seabed
The dentin string flutters and
Growing daisies on its back
Sways in the wind
This may be the stain of attack by a crochet needle
Shapes of a deer's hoof prints remain
Pieces of gold leaf flutter to the ground
The sound of red coral
Piled high on top of a thicket's talkativeness
A stone pagoda
The scream that vomits drowned air
Becomes blurry
And the fragility of dried leaves continually deposited
Smoothly
Tilts
Calling to mind a gentle footpath through the rice fields
Standing still, stoically, at a junction of three roads
As if hanging suspended
To wait upon, to serve
Longing for a thatched roof
Steam is always hanging around
Without a hitch
Without mishap
Voice of one whose name is unknown
Name straddling the railroad ties

Translated by Eric Selland

鳩の姿をした待ち人から滴る汗、
拭う、
冴えない頭のなかの平凡な丘の覚醒を求めて、
冷たい慕情に凭れかかって、
いまにも倒れてしまいそうな脆弱さ、
浚われて、
篩われた泥、
眩い、
白銀の馬が何頭も駆けてくる、
馭者は、
松明を掲げて朝の輪郭をなぞる、
円筒形の隧道をぬけて、
光を帯びた快い球体、
爽やかな火焔、
玻璃がとりまく、
ただちに排泄をすませて、
洗濯板の歪んだ螢光燈を、
交換せよ、
交換せよ、

Covered in snow of ritual purification
Sweat drips from people waiting in the appearance of doves
Wiping the sweat away
To seek awakening on a commonplace hill amongst the weak-minded
Leaning against cold affection
So fragile it could collapse at any moment
Then it's snatched away
Mud passed through a sieve
How pretty
Silvery white horses come galloping over
The riders
Carry torches and follow the contour of morning
They pass through a cylindrical tunnel
A delectable sphere tinged with light
An invigorating blaze
Surrounded by crystal
Excretion is quickly dispensed with
And the fluorescent light on a distorted washboard—
Replace it!
Replace it!

Translated by Eric Selland

ŌSAKI SAYAKA was born in Tokyo in 1982. Since debuting in 2011, she has become one of the leading poets of her generation. She describes herself as a "badger-like girl" who loves to produce handmade books, write poems, and stay in constant motion.

炊飯器

いちばんすきな画家がいたはずなのに　忘れてしまった
いちばんすきな歌があったはずなのに　忘れてしまった
しかたがないから　炊飯器でごはんを炊いた
炊飯器なんかすきじゃないのに

自分の生まれた日の天気を　誰も知らない
自分の生まれた日に死んだ人とは　会話できない
あとから誰かが教えた話を信じることにして
トイレットペーパーが切れたので　探しにいく

抵抗するための手段を探しているうちに　夜になっていた
生き延びるのに夢中になっているうちに　朝になっていた
何を言いかけていたのか　思いだせなかったから
目の前で息をしているあなたの手を握った

あなたがノートの見開きに書きとめることばと
わたしが本で読んで泣いたことばは　ちがう
あなたはおかしいと思うかもしれないけど
わたしはそのことが　嬉しすぎて笑えた

Translated by
JEFFREY ANGLES

Rice Steamer

I used to have a favorite artist but I forgot who it was
I used to have a favorite song but I forgot what it was
Not sure what to do, I cooked some rice in the steamer
Even though I don't like those damn machines

No one knows the weather on the day they were born
No one can talk with people who died the day they were born
I decide to put my faith in something someone told me
The toilet paper has run out so I go look for some more

Night falls as I am looking for a means of resistance
Morning dawns as I am preoccupied with living long
I forgot what I was going to say so I took your hand
You who were breathing, right there in front of me

The words you write across the pages of your notebook
Are not the same as the words in the book which made me cry
You might think it is strange but that thought
Made me so happy I laughed out loud

I will probably say whatever I want
About the weather on the day you were born
I will probably exaggerate and make mistakes
About the people who died the day you were born

あなたの生まれた日の天気を
わたしはわたしの好きなように語るだろう
あなたの生まれた日に死んだ人のことも
誇張したり間違えたりしながら語るだろう
あなたははじめわたしの話をぜんぶ信じて驚き
それからあまりすぐには信じないことにするだろう

あなたがわたしを信じないことが
炊飯器と暮らすわたしを勇気づける
すきな絵を忘れてもわたしは平気だろう
自分の野蛮な魂に自信をもつだろう

広げたブルーシートのうえに
持ち寄ったおにぎりや日用品を並べて
お花見みたいだねと言いながら
あなたは生きている

At first, you'll be shocked and believe me completely
Soon you'll decide not to trust me so readily

The fact you won't trust me gives me courage
As I live here with my rice steamer
I'm fine even though I forget the paintings I love
I have faith in my savage soul

We spread out a blue plastic sheet and on it
We line up the rice balls and other things we brought home
You say it's like we're picnicking under the cherry blossoms
And as you do, you live

Translated by Jeffrey Angles

ゆっくりと流れる世界の粒子

冬の朝、最後の一葉は枝を離れて落ちる
ヘルメットをかぶった人たちが調査に出て
そのほかの出来事をみんな見逃す
見逃しながら、その利き手に
その日の労働を握りしめる

キツネが森の奥を通ったのも
観測所の日陰の霜柱をリスが踏んだのも
誰も見なかった
漁師の捨てた魚をヒグマが食べたのも
誰も見なかった（ことにした）
ヘルメットをかぶった人たちは
かもしかの糞に木の実が混ざっているのを見るだけで
お行儀よく満足した

真面目な人たちは記録した
私はアンデルセンのパンを食べてた
勤勉な人たちは陽当たりを考慮して伐採した
私は買ってきたゲームをやってた

Slowly Flowing Particles of the World

Winter morning, the last leaf falls from its branch
Helmeted people come to conduct surveys
And overlook everything else
Meanwhile, they hold the day's labor
Tight in their dominant hand

No one notices
The fox sauntering through the forest depths
The squirrel treading on icy frost in the shade below the observatory
The fish the fisherman discards and a brown bear gobbles down
No one notices (or so it seemed to me)
The people in helmets
Took polite satisfaction
Merely noticing the fruit in the antelope feces

The serious ones make notes
I was eating some bread from a bakery
The hardest workers felled trees, thinking of sunlight
I played a game I'd brought
What passed us in the meantime?
No one noticed

In addition to the visible
Invisible particles slowly
Flowed by

Translated by Jeffrey Angles

その間に何が通りすぎていったか
誰も見なかった

見えるもののほかは
そこらじゅう見えなかった
ゆっくりと粒子は流れていった
月が昼を通りすぎた
細い草がのほうずに生え
人も動物もいなくなった場所では
わかれていた世界が閉じて
見るものと見られるものの区別がなくなった

誰もがたいてい何かを見ていた
それでたいてい何かを見逃していた
見えないものは片っ端から言葉にされた
誰かが水のなかにゼラチンをいれてかき混ぜ
言葉にして見えるようにした
そして見えるようにしたものを見逃してばかりいた

粒子はゆっくりと見えないまま流れていった
よいものでも
わるいものでもなく
誰かの命の源となり
誰かのからだの毒となり
ただ一緒にはびこって
元気にほかのいっさいを滅ぼし
お互いを許しあう関係を探しながら

The moon passed through afternoon
Thin blades of grass grew wild
Where there were no more people or animals
The divided world closed its doors
Collapsing the distinction
Between those who see
And those who are seen

Almost everyone saw something
Almost everyone overlooked something
One by one, the invisible was transformed into words
Someone stirred gelatin into water
Transformed it into language, made it visible
Then simply overlooked what now she could see

Slowly the particles, still invisible, flowed on
Not necessarily good
Not necessarily bad
Becoming the source of someone's life
Becoming the poison in someone's body
Growing rampant together
They kill all else
While still seeking one another's forgiveness

Translated by Jeffrey Angles

MIZUHO ISHIDA travels widely and writes poetry in conversation with international culture and current events. After the 2011 earthquake and tsunami, he conducted several interviews with people in the affected area, including his hometown, Saitama, where he is the head priest of the Enzo-in Buddhist temple.

月の犬

乾いた凍土に舌をたらすと　犬たちはハアハア
歩きまわり、次々　荒野を生みだしてゆく。
空になにか白いものを見つけて、彼女は
　それを月だと教わった。
他郷の響きにはアドレスがない。
昨日の白が裂けて、耳鳴りの内奥から
新しい悲鳴が咲きだす。世間とは肌理の
つながりで　生きていく。それだけ。

　都会のスーパーから部屋に帰る
仏壇に飾られた遺影、徹底された無言。
　ボイスレコーダーの電子音と
紙のふれあう音、母が子の爪を切る鋏のリズムが
　ぱちん　ち　ち
ぱちん　ちち　ぱちん　ち　宙に
鳥たちのさえずりや羽音みたく漂っていた。

無音の霧のなかで耳を澄ますとどうしても
だれもいない村に帰ってきてしまう。
　黒とブルーの防護服に身を包み、

Translated by
JUDY HALEBSKY AND TOMOYUKI ENDO

Moon Dog

Putting their tongues down to the frozen ground
dogs walk about panting *hah, hah*, creating a
no-man's-land.
Finding something white up in the sky,
she learns that it's the moon.
There is no address with the sound of no-man's-land.
Yesterday's moon torn out of the sky.
In my head, a ceaseless humming.
In the world outside of this skin
a new moon. That's all.

Coming back from a supermarket downtown
the portraits of the ancestors, the absolute silence.

白いマスクとヘルメットで顔をおおった作業員たち。
屋敷門のある築二百年のタカん家は除染車により
しゅー、しゅー、茅葺屋根から丸ごと
薬液を吹きかけられている。

二年と三月の不在の力学、あわあわした黄色の
穂先たちが　ビニールハウスの
天井をつきやぶり　パイプ鉄骨を持ちあげていた。
牛たちの消えた牛舎には、
黒いビニール袋の山が積み上げられている。
六月の田畑は一面　シロツメグサの静かな白い瞳で、
きっちゃんが後を継いだ駄菓子屋は
「資材館」とひとことそっけなく
看板があり、児童公園は銀色のタンクの林になった。

雀をガス欠にしてやるんだと息巻いた
ＢＢ弾のレンジャー、ピアノが上手で礼儀正しい
ミツコはどこへいった。家の前を通ると、
野球中継と喧嘩と猫の声が
とびかっていたサエキ兄弟は?
遊び仲間のいる十字路で、するどく口笛を吹いても
夕方の陽気な世界に飛びだす子は

Floating in the air, the recorder's electric hum
the rustling of papers, the rhythm of the mother
clipping her son's nails
ptinc, tic, tic,
ptinc, titic, ptinc, tic...
up in the sky, a distant flapping of birds.

Within the fog of silence, hearing nothing
I come back to no-man's village.
Laborers in black and blue radiation suits protecting their bodies,
covering their faces with white masks, their heads with helmets.
Taka's farmhouse with its two-hundred-year-old gate
the whole thing washed by some chemical spray
shh, shh...

Power grids of nonexistence,
two years and three months in this no-man's-land.
The tips of sallow, foamy plants have broken through
the tops of the greenhouses.
They have lifted the iron frames that held the glass in place.
Now, in the barns with no cows
there are piled mountains of black plastic bags.
The paddies and fields in June are covered
with eyes of white clover.
Kit'chan took over the penny candy store
has a sign that simply says, *WAREHOUSE*
and the children's park turned to a grove of huge silver tanks.

A boy playing park ranger with his BB gun
declaring, *those sparrows, I'm gonna smoke 'em!*
Where is Mitsuko, our polite and tender piano player?
What happened to the Saeki brothers?
Passing their house, I would always hear

ひとりもいない。
幻種の蝶のように　家々の戸板にひらひら舞う
避難先住所とケータイ番号は
奪われたどの未来や過去にもつながっていない。

酔ったコガの爺さまがテレビカメラに言いはなつ
あんたらはねえ　瓦礫、瓦礫いうけど
わたしたちの先祖代々が暮らした家なんだ。
おれにはいえん、そんなふうに
いっちゃあ、いかんよ。
よどで　ばらばらになっても
木っ端になったって、ふる里ですから。

それでも彼女は泣いたのではなかった
泣くこともできないくらい深く哀しんで
体から透明なしずくを一粒あふれさせただけだった。
ふるえる、液体という音響伝達器
涙は語るのだ。
そのあまりに密やかな音は
どんな言葉にも届いてはいないけれど—。

quarrels and meowing and the baseball game on TV.
At the corner, where there should be lots of people out
there's a sharp whistling
nobody comes into the glimmering dusk.
All there is
is a new species of butterfly
the evacuation addresses and cell phone numbers
fluttering on the doors of houses
not connected to the future or the past.

The grandpa at Koga's, drunk, shouts at the TV camera,
You call this debris? These are the parts of the house
where our ancestors lived.
I can't call this garbage
and you can't either.
What the tsunami has turned into rubble,
this is my home.

And then, there's the young mother who doesn't cry.
She sighs deeply, in equal measure.
From her body, one transparent drop,
quavering, sound-transmitting.
This tear speaks
but the sound is too weak to reach any word.

She hurriedly tries to hold the whispers of her memories
lost and almost lost
ptinc, tic, tic, ptinc, titic, ptinc, tic
just like she holds her son, sleepless in the rain,
by the restful song of the clipper.

From the little finger on his left hand
one by one, slowly, and carefully
not to make a mistake

若い母親は　みなし児になってしまいそうな
　記憶の囁きを急いで抱きしめる。
ぱちん　ぱちん　ちち　ぱち　ち
雨がこわくて眠れない子を 安らぎにみちた
　鋏の歌で　抱きしめるみたいに。

左手の小指から順番に　ゆっくり　慎重に
まちがえずに　爪切りを動かしていく
もうすぐ　こんなふうに　ていねいに
　切らせてはもらえなくなるから。

おさない爪はまだやわらかく　澄んでいて
　鋭く輝く刃をあてるとかんたんに
はなれ　こぼれ　いくつもの透明な月が、
　海も潮騒もない連絡ノートの
まっさらな水平線にはらはら落ちてゆく。
　　夜の底に
　　このひとときを封印する
　　鍵音のように響いて。

working the clipper.
Soon, she won't have the chance to
clip his nails.

The nails are still soft and transparent.
They are easily clipped and fall
and so many transparent moons fall
one after another
on the clear horizon of a handwritten note
without sea or the sound of the waves
sounding as a piano key
sealing this moment into the deep bottom of the sea.

Translated by Judy Halebsky and Tomoyuki Endo

WAGŌ RYŌICHI is a Fukushima native. At the time of the nuclear meltdown, he gained national attention by publishing poetry from the disaster zone on Twitter. He now uses his platform as Fukushima's best-known writer to campaign for the region and the antinuclear movement.

廃炉詩篇

「廃炉まで四十年」（現時点）

ところでわたしの言葉の

原子炉を廃炉にするには

何年かかる

のだろう

この地球を　この虹を　この雲を

この指先の棘を

廃炉にするには　どれぐらいか

エネルギーのささやきを耳にしながら惑うばかりだ

ああ

今日の言葉を廃炉にするには

何十年かかるのだろうか

水平線はいつも真っ直ぐなままだ

しだいに明るくなる

夜の廃炉が終わったのだ

Psalm to a Decommissioned Reactor

Translated by
JEFFREY ANGLES

“forty years until the reactor is decommissioned” (at present)
    but in my language
    how many years will it take
                    to replace the word *reactor*
                        with *decommissioned reactor*

how long
    to replace this earth, this rainbow, this cloud
                    the thorns of this fingerprint
                        with a decommissioned reactor

listening to whispers of energy, I lose my way
oh!
how many decades will it take
            until *decommissioned reactor* is the word of the day

                    the horizon over the sea is always perfectly straight

●●●

狂った水平線はいつも在る
ある日のわたしが思い浮べる想像の果てに
ある日のわたしがわたしであることの運命の隣に

ある日のわたしの親友が帳面にすっと線を引いた　そこに
ある日のわたしが知る何億光年も先の乾いた星の感情に
ある日のわたしが箸でつまみそこねた豆粒の先に

ある日のわたしがくしゃくしゃに丸めた白い地図の裏に
ある日のわたしが泣きながら髪を洗って目を閉じている時　その無垢な背中のどこかに
ある日のわたしが笑ったあとの　一抹の寂しさの中に　真っ直ぐに真横に
さっき　青空に　稲妻が走ったが　そこに

ある日のわたしは激怒して本を破き　壁に何枚もの紙片をそこに投げつけて
泣きわめいていたが　その時に気狂いに　何頁にもそこに
ある日のわたしは腕時計を一分だけ早めたがそこに
ある日のわたしはわたしであることの意味をわたしに問い直しているうちに
ある日のわたしはわたしをすっかりと愛してしまった　うなずくとそこに

ある日のわたしは全てを奪われたまま　遠くのやりきれなさを
海岸線を行く一台のトラックの影に見ているが　その向こうに
狂った水平線はいつも在る
狂った水平線はいつも真っ直ぐである

わたしたちの記憶の奥底で海亀が反転している　指

it grows gradually lighter
the reactor of night has cleased its operations

●●●

there is always an uneven horizon over the sea
at the ends of my imagination
    one particular day
next to the dictates of fate that I be myself
    one particular day
there, in the line that a dear friend drew so smoothly in my notebook
    one particular day
in the dried-up star hundreds of millions of light years away I learned about
    one particular day
beyond the beans that I tried to pick up with chopsticks
    one particular day

を無くしたわたしの猿は
足跡を黄金色にして歯を剥き出しにして　英語を忘れている
わたしの脳髄
で燃え盛る電信柱をどうにかしたまえ　蛸の影がわたしを
追い抜いていくのだ
恐ろしい荒海
の三月某日に　真っ青なポップコーンが
思想の奥で弾けていたことを思い出すのだ　許
されない宇宙の待合室の闇で
飛行機の飛ばない思想の滑走路をどうにかしたまえ
そこを船と車と津波がやっ
て来たあの日
ところで地図の表に地図のな
い日がやって来た
無意味な言葉の太平洋に
狂った水平線はいつも在る
燃えあがる紙コップのイメージを
わたしたちは消し潰すこと
など出来ないのだ
ある日は　飴を嘗めながら馬が溶けていくのだ
だから忘却を忘れてしまえ
タンカーの給油は停止　ある日は雲と霰とが歩いてきた
わたしたちの中にはまだはっきりと震災がある
あの日から起立し続けている紫色の電信柱の影に

on the white backside of the map I crumpled up
    one particular day
on my son's innocent back as I washed his hair, his eyes closed and weeping
    one particular day
in the front-on view, in the profile, in my small sadness after laughing a little,
    one particular day
in the path of the lightning flashing just now across the blue sky

in my anger, in the countless sheets when I flew into a rage, tore up a book
& threw the scraps of paper at the wall, wailing out loud
    one particular day
in setting my wristwatch one minute ahead
    one particular day
in asking myself once again what meaning there is in being me
    one particular day
in nodding over how much I used to love myself
    one particular day
in everything that has been ripped away from me
    one particular day

無言の電気の進軍を恐怖する
狂ったわたしが顔中に太陽を貼り
ああ　たったいま静かに朝
日に沈んでゆくのか
大粒の岩塩を左目の尻からこぼして
拳で拭うしかないのか
巨大な平目
がはるかな生命からやって来る
独り言は沈黙に満潮と干潮とを与
えるのだろうか
狂った水平線はいつも在る 真っ直ぐに　ある
見たまえ　感性の暴力的な　岩場を
しぶきをあげている　非在なる地球の影を
残酷なわたしたちの頭脳を白い川が流れてい
く
近所の真っ赤な屋根をどうすればいいのか
午前四時はどうしようもない姿で午前五
時になるのか
頭の中でそびえ立つ野原の鉄塔
記憶の真ん中で奪い去られる堅牢な日常
靴の中で遊ぶ何千もの子どもたちの影
誰もいない湾岸道路のまばらな林で
火だるまになったフクロウの影が
ヌレネズミになったミミズクの影を追い抜くと
かつて煙

in distant disgust, I watch the shadow of a truck tracing the horizon
beyond that, there is always an uneven horizon over the sea
the always uneven horizon
is always straight ahead
the sea turtles in the deepest
recesses of our memory have overturned
having lost
its fingers, my monkey

leaves golden footprints,
bears its teeth, forgets English
do something about
the electrical towers blazing
inside my brain the shadow of an octopus
overtakes me
in the terrifying roughness
of the sea that day in March
I remember
bright blue popcorn bursting

をあげた発電所ではイメージの廃炉がさらに進まなくなっていく　二十キロ
圏内で
誰かが狂った扇風機を修理したからだ
朝焼けが迫ってくるぞ　逃げなくていいのか
黄金虫の
夢で無人の大型バスは横転している
感覚の未明に
生まれたばかりの浅蜊に砂を吐かせ
ると
真実は港の電信柱の長い柔らかな影になって
二匹の九官鳥は三匹になったまま八匹にな
り九匹
片方の靴を無くした少年が
背負っているものは
巨大な平目の影だ
はるかな生命からやって
来たのだ
狂ったー直線はいつも在る
狂ったー直線はいつも真っ直ぐにある
頭の後ろで
南半球の風車が
燃えながら回っているから
回っているから　もうじき朝が来るのだ
光の波

in the depths of our beliefs
in unforgiving darkness
of the waiting
room of the universe
do something about the runways of our belief systems
where airplanes no longer fly
that's where the boats, cars,
& tsunami crashed ashore that day
the day arrived
when on the front of the map
the map was no more
"Pacific Ocean" became meaningless words
there is always an uneven horizon over the sea

I cannot suppress
the images of
those burning paper cups
one day horses will dissolve
while licking their sweets

Translated by Jeffrey Angles

わたしたちの言葉の洪水が襲うのは　わたしたちの言葉の街路　言葉の港湾　言葉の国道
言葉の横腹　水しぶきに泣き叫ぶ人々の声と　車と家と電信柱と火星とボールペンと金星と
前世に無くした手袋が　観念の春の浜辺へと打ち上げられているのが分かったのか

そして水平線は
真っ直ぐのまま
折れ曲がるのだ

そしてあるいは
折れ曲がらない
夜明けの廃炉へ

so forget all about oblivion
no more refueling tankers
one day clouds & mist came walking in

the disasters are certainly still within us

in the purple shade of the electrical towers
springing up constantly since that day
I fear the advancing army
of silent electricity
I stick the sun on
my crazed countenance
ahhh! is the morning
sun silently setting right now?

is my only choice
to use my fist to wipe away
the large lump of rock salt

Translated by Jeffrey Angles

spilling from my left eye?

with its flat eyes
the giant flounder
comes from a distant source of life

will these words whispered to myself
bring tides, high & low,
to silence?

the horizon over the sea is always uneven
it is always straight ahead
just look at the violent, rocky shores
at the jets of spray
at the shadows of an earth that does not exist
white rivers flow through our cruel brains

what should we do about the red roofs
in our neighborhoods?
will 4 am just roll around to 5 as if nothing

can be done?
metal towers rising precipitously
in the fields inside our heads
the durable everyday in the middle
of memories taken away
the shadows of thousands of children
playing in their shoes
in the sparse woods off a coastal road
where no one walks
the shadow of an owl turned into sparks
overtakes the shadow of a horned owl
turned into a wet mouse
right then, at the power plant
that once let out smoke
the decommissioned reactors in our imaginations stop

someone has repaired the crazy fan
with the 20 km radius

Translated by Jeffrey Angles

dawn is approaching don’t you want to run away
in a gold-bug dream?
a large, empty bus lies on its side
before the dawn of sensation
a newborn clam spits out sand
the truth becomes a long, soft
shadow of an electric pole in the port
two mynah birds become three
eight then nine
a young man who has lost one of his shoes
is carrying on his back
the shadow of a giant flounder
which has come from
a distant source of life
there is always an uneven line
the uneven line is always straight ahead
at the backs of our imaginations

windmills in the southern hemisphere
are burning as they turn soon dawn will come
a wave of light

the floods of our language assault the pathways of our language the gulfs of language the highways of language spills over the sides of language the voices of people weeping & calling out in the sprays of water cars & houses & electrical poles & Mars & ball-point pens & Venus & even the gloves I lost in my previous life don't you realize that all these things have washed up on the spring shores of our ideals?

and then the horizon over the sea
still straight
begins to bend
toward the decommissioned reactor at dawn
but then again
maybe it does not

Contributors

JEFFREY ANGLES is a professor at Western Michigan University. His Japanese-language poetry collection *Watashi no hizukehenkōsen* (My International Date Line) won the highly coveted Yomiuri Prize for Literature in 2017, making him the first non-native speaker ever to win this award for poetry. He is also the award-winning translator of dozens of Japan's most important writers. His most recent translation is of the modernist novel *The Book of the Dead* by Orikuchi Shinobu.

JOE DELONG is a writing lecturer at Case Western Reserve University. His poetry has appeared in journals such as *Denver Quarterly*, *Nimrod*, *Puerto del Sol*, *Mid-American Review*, *Redactions*, and *Mantis*. In his translation of "Circle," "Kasumi" refers to Kasumigaseki, an area containing offices of numerous Japanese government institutions.

TED DODSON is the author of the poetry collection *At the National Monument / Always Today* (Pioneer Works, 2016). He's a contributing editor for *BOMB*, an editor of *Futurepoem*, and the former editor of the *Poetry Project Newsletter*.

ELLEN ELIAS-BURSAĆ translates novels and nonfiction by Bosnian, Croatian, and Serbian writers. She was awarded ALTA's National Translation Award for her translation of David Albahari's novel *Götz and Meyer* in 2006.

TOMOYUKI ENDO is an assistant professor at Wako University in Tokyo. He teaches poetry of the twentieth century, ranging from work by Ezra Pound, William Carlos Williams, Gary Snyder, Nishiwaki Junzaburō, Kitasono Katsue, and Miyazawa Kenji to the lyrics of popular music by The Beatles, Simon and Garfunkel, Bob Dylan, Bob Marley, and others. He is also a co-translator, with Forrest Gander, of Kazuko Shiraishi's *My Floating Mother, City* (New Directions), and loves to cook.

EDWARD GAUVIN has received fellowships and residencies from PEN America, the NEA, the Fulbright program, the Lannan Foundation, and the French Embassy. Other publications have appeared in the *New York Times*, *Harper's*, *World Literature Today*, and *Weird Fiction Review*. The translator of three hundred graphic novels, he is a contributing editor for comics at *Words Without Borders*. His translation of Georges-Olivier Châteaureynaud's novella *The Messengers* is forthcoming from Wakefield Press in Spring 2019.

JUDY HALEBSKY is the author of *Tree Line* and *Sky=Empty,* which won the New Issues Poetry Prize. Her honors include fellowships from the MacDowell Colony, the Millay Colony, and the Vermont Studio Center. As a Japanese Ministry of Culture (MEXT) scholar, she trained in Japanese Noh theater at Hosei University in Tokyo. She teaches English and creative writing at Dominican University of California and lives in Oakland.

NORIKO HARA has received degrees from the University of Tokyo and the University of Pittsburgh. She has taught at the University of Cincinnati, and she currently lives in Japan.

SHOHREH LAICI (born in 1986) is a Tehran-based author and literary translator. Her works are forthcoming in *Asheville Poetry Review* and *Ezra: An Online Journal of Translation*. Besides her literary works, Shohreh has produced a variety of video art and performance art pieces exploring the notion of femininity, language, and social taboos. Her controversial performance art, titled "Hills Like White Elephants," loosely based on Ernest Hemingway's short story, explored the concept of abortion in Iranian patriarchal society.

NOAH M. MINTZ met Patrick Goujon while taking his creative writing workshop in Paris, and began translating *À l'arrache* through ALTA's Emerging Translator Mentorship. Noah got his BA in French and media studies at Vassar College, and spent two years selling books in San Francisco, where he also sat on the jury for the French consulate's "Room with a View" residency. He recently moved to New York to pursue a PhD in French at Columbia University.

ACHY OBEJAS is a writer, journalist, and translator. She is the author of five books of fiction and has translated Junot Díaz and Wendy Guerra, among many others. She is from Cuba and lives in California.

ANNA ROSENWONG's translation of Rocío Cerón's *Diorama* won the Best Translated Book Award, and a collection of José Eugenio Sánchez's poems, *Here the Sun's for Real*, is forthcoming. She has received fellowships from the NEA, the Banff International Literary Translation Centre, and the American Literary Translators Association, and is the translation editor of *Anomaly*. Her work has been featured in such venues as *World Literature Today*, *The Kenyon Review*, and *Modern Poetry Today*. More at annarosenwong.com.

ERIC SELLAND is the author of *The Condition of Music* (Sink Press), *Arc Tangent*, and *Beethoven's Dream* (both from Isobar Press, Tokyo). His translation of *The Guest Cat*, a novel by Takashi Hiraide, was on the *New York Times* best-seller list in February of 2014. Eric currently lives in Tokyo where he works as a translator of economic reports.

TIMEA SIPOS is a Hungarian-American writer and translator, currently earning her MFA in fiction at The University of Nevada, Las Vegas, where she is an instructor and an intern at *The Believer*. A 2017 American Literary Translators Association Travel Fellow, her work has appeared or is forthcoming in *The Offing*, *The Short Story Project*, *Juked*, and elsewhere. You can follow her on Twitter: @timearozalia

MARCELA SULAK's poetry collections include *Decency* (2015) and *Immigrant*. She's co-edited *Family Resemblance: An Anthology and Exploration of 8 Hybrid Literary Genres*. Her fourth book-length poetry translation, *Twenty Girls to Envy Me: Selected Poems of Orit Gidali* (University of Texas Press), was longlisted for the 2017 PEN Award for Poetry in Translation. She hosts the TLV.1 radio podcast "Israel in Translation," edits *The Ilanot Review*, and is associate professor of literature at Bar-Ilan University.

KYOKO YOSHIDA is a fiction writer and a translator. Her collection of short stories *Disorientalism* came out from Vagabond Press in Sydney, and her stories appear in *BooksActually's Gold Standard 2016* (Singapore), *After Coetzee* (Faunary Press, Minneapolis), and others. She has co-translated Kiwao Nomura (*Spectacle & Pigsty*) and Gōzō Yoshimasu with poet Forrest Gander, as well as Masataka Matsuda and Shu Matsui with playwright Andy Bragen. She has also translated Dave Eggers and Gary Shteyngart into Japanese.

Credits

Note: All author names from "The Japanese Vanguard" are formatted according to the author's preference. In the citations below, all author names appear last name first.

ALBAHARI, DAVID. In *Kontrolni punkt.* Belgrade: Stubovi culture, 2011.

ARJOUNI, NAHID. "Kitchen God," "Refugee Camp," "Deaden," and "My roots were somewhere with you" in *No One Takes a Photograph of Our Saturdays.* Arbil, Iraq: Aras Publisher, 2011–12.

CERÓN, ROCÍO. "America" in *Tiento.* San Nicolás de los Garza, Mexico: Universidad autónoma de Nuevo León, 2010.

CHÂTEAUREYNAUD, GEORGES-OLIVIER. "Une route poudreuse mène d'Argos à Mycènes" in *Jeune vieillard assis sur une pierre en bois.* Paris: Éditions Grasset & Fasquelle, 2013.

ENOMOTO, SACLACO. "ANADYOMENE" in *Zōshoku suru gankyū ni matagatte.* Tokyo: Shichōsha, 2012.

GOUJON, PATRICK. In *À l'arrache.* Paris: Gallimard, 2011.

HACHIKAI, MIMI. "Samayou niwa o samayou" in *Kao o arau mizu.* Tokyo: Shichōsha, 2015. "Kū mono wa kuwareru yoru" and "Nijū no yokubō" in *Kūmono wa kuwareru yoru.* Tokyo: Shichōsha, 2005.

HASS, SHARRON. "Dinner with Joachim" in *Ha-oryom* [Daylight]. Jerusalem: The Bialik Institute, 2011.

INDIANA, RITA. In *La mucama de Omicunlé.* Cáceres, Spain: Editorial Periférica, 2015.

ISHIDA, MIZUHO. "Moon Dog" in *Ear, Bamboo Leaf Boat.* Tokyo: Shichousha, 2015.

ŌSAKI, SAYAKA. "Suihanki" in *Atarashii sumika.* Tokyo: Seidosha, 2018. "Yukkuri to nagareru sekai no ryūshi" in *Yubisasu koto ga dekinai.* Tokyo: Seidosha, 2014.

PAPP-ZAKOR, ILKA. "Anyuka" in *Angyalvacsora.* Budapest: József Attila Kör, Prae.hu, 2015.

SÁENZ, JAIME. "Muerte por el tacto" in *El frío / Muerte por el tacto / Aniversario de una vision.* La Paz, Bolivia: Editorial Burillo, 1967.

SASŌ, KEN'ICHI. "Gesshoku," "Ikiteiru no desu," and "Wakka" in *Mori no namioto.* Tokyo: Coal Sack, 2015.

WAGŌ, RYŌICHI. "Hairo shihen" in *Hairo shihen.* Tokyo: Shichōsha, 2013.

Index by Language